To Ste

You might enjoy one or two of the jokes.

# ECSTASY IN THE EVENING

### By JFR Stableford

*In homage to The Master*

To JR Stableford

**By the same author**

*Several books.*

PLUMMIE BOOKS 2024

## A Note On Names

*This is my stab at the truth, but a few legally-minded clever-clogses have urged me to smudge around a few of the actual names, for fear of crushing legal fees. As an obliging kind of a dude, what could I do? Other names have been left oh-natural, and I also remain, pretty sincerely,*

**Banjo Wako x**

## Chapter One

"Hey, Suri?"

*"What can I help you with?"*

"Ah, right. Well, what's the weather like tonight?"

*"Okay, I found this on the web for, 'Find my nearest surf shack'! Check it out..."*

"Oh, cancel, stop."

*"...Okay, what's next?"*

"Search 'How to write a book'."

*"I'm sorry, I'm having difficulty accessing the network."*

"Oh, Jeeesus Joplin, Suri, will you please explain to me how it's possible to squeeze into one volume the sphincter-strangling melodrama of Yaxley Castle, the fruity portrait, the Buck-Up special brew, and the massive ugly racist – a sweaty tangle of peril which nearly plunged the last of the Wakos hairline-deep in the hottest of hot shit soup?"

*"Okay, I found this on the web for, 'Shih Tzu breeders'! Check it out..."*

"Oh, forget it."

*"Okay, I found this on the web for, 'forklift trucks'! Check it out..."*

Have you ever felt you were lacking a guardian angel? For want of a less God-flavoured term? I try to see myself as, I hope, in all the ways that count, a proper stand-up member of society, at least independently capable of tying my shoelaces when it's not flip-flop weather, and qualified to successfully wipe myself where and when necessary. I should also imagine that most folk who know me will tell you that few dudes are less inclined to whine about their lot in life than Banjo Wako. Slinking through existence with a smile never less than a flicker away from my lips, enjoying the 'bella vitae' however it comes, spreading the love and chuckles on thick wherever I go, has always been my preferred path.

I think it's fair to say that I have never found myself short of friends, whose calamitous lives I am of course positively delirious to improve however I can. But as I look back, I can definitely see times when what would have been really quite welcome was the arrival of the aforementioned G.A. – some kind of guru, a higher power, a wise watcher who would have been able to, I don't know, nudge me in the right direction when push came to shove-right-in-the-face, and increase the volume of sweetness and light in my biography.

That's a phrase which has stuck with me, and in me, for maybe forever – 'Sweetness and Light', 'Sweetness and Light' – it seems to sum it all up somehow. I do spend my existence trying my best to spread the maximum amount of S and L, and it can be an exhausting job, when working solo.

I don't like to overthink things. My Auntie Akifa would say I barely think at all. Therefore, the last thing I want to do is get bogged down in "biography", this book project is a bit of a diversion for me, gabbing away in text in this way. Tweeting always seemed like too much bother, let alone all this.

If you want my writer's CV, there was that time when my Auntie Faiza roped me in to write a guest blog for her lifestyle site, *Woman Stuff* – yes, readers from the West Midlands, my younger auntie is Faiza Malone, the legendary purring tiger veteran reporter for *Midlands This Evening* for the last quarter century or more – not that she'd thank me for putting it that way. Becoming a TV News broadcaster was always Auntie Faiza's dream, as her adoring public will attest – though few of her fans realise that the second my auntie signs off in her famous sultry tones and the broadcast cuts back to the studio, she slips back into her real voice, a foghorn which has been known to make turtles' ears bleed on the shores of California. Having arrived in the Black Country so young, Faiza's real speaking – well, shouting – voice somewhat puts me in mind of Noddy Holder, making himself heard over a jet engine, after you've stamped on his foot.

Anyway, 'How To Dress As Yourself', my little offering was called. I do dig clothes, you see. I wouldn't call myself the shallowest biped in town, but you have to agree, clothes do matter. Your outer shell protects the wobbly bits inside, and there's no harm in broadcasting something to make the eyes pop with your limb casings. Apparently my ramblings about the importance of avoiding Superdry and whatnot drew a fair number of hits and encouraging comments for Auntie Faiza's web site – but that aside, rhyme, not prose, has always been my favoured bag of goodies.

I'm trying to avoid biographical bogginess, as I say, but returning to my theme, the first time I felt the lack of what we're calling a G.A. – the guardian angel, you know – was probably back when I first popped out, in the summer of 1987, in the Sudanese city of Juba. Specifically, in a small ladies toilet which failed to keep out the rat-a-tat of street battles riddling the neighbourhood outside. For those like me who spent their Geography lessons colouring in band logos rather than learning the average rainfall in Minsk, you'll find Sudan – or rather, Southern Sudan, as it now is, the world's youngest country – about halfway down the right hand side of Africa, squidged next to Ethiopia. Not a stroll away.

Frankly, my Auntie Akifa – four-foot-eight of barbed-wire-bra-wearing Christian napalm – tells this story much better than me. Her well-rehearsed version is packed with grumbling cries to God aplenty, but the story always ends the same way:

"...And then it all happened at once, boy – out you damn came with a gush of froth, and you made your laugh-cry, and all at once – *oh, Lord!* – once she held you in her arms – *oh, Jehovah!* – and she called you Benjamin – *oh, my poor Laila!* – your poor dashed mother sighed, 'The worst is over now', and she left us for a pair of wings..."

Oh, and there was her usual finale, "...and now I find you STEALING, boy, STEALING your own auntie's blessed liquorice allsorts!"

Auntie Akifa's retellings of this tale tended to come any time she felt the need to remind me that my very existence came at a price to which I would never be able to stretch – and when I was small, the familiar saga was often broken up by her own brand of physical punctuation, AKA a good clouting. I never questioned this capital treatment, my auntie was and is old school, freely using her fat open hands for emphasis around the back of my fat open head when the mood took her. She drummed – if drummed is the word I'm grasping for – one thing into me, from toddlerhood onwards – "INTEGRATE! INTEGRATE!" like some form of refugee Dalek. "RESPECT!" was another word she used more often than Aretha Franklyn's backing singers, telling me, "There's the Lord up in heaven, and the Lord up in the castle, and you show your respect to them both, my boy. We are dashed lucky that here we have the Police constabulary, we have law and order, we have the Church, God bless it, and we have Lords and we have Dames of the British Empire, and we live in a happy land! Be grateful for it all, Benjamin."

These days when not watching the racing she mainly just grumbles away to her fuzzy familiar, an eternally yappy Pekingese named Apple, who nestles into her bosom with googly eyes popping out upon every squeeze of Auntie Akifa's zealous emphasis.

Though it's been many years since I felt the rough edge of the back and front of her hand, Auntie Akifa's word has generally remained law. I make no secret of the fact that she can still turn me into a puddle of gabbling gloop with one glare to this day – me and many a grown man, I don't know of anyone not terrified of her. Akifa Wako has a stare which would tie Medusa's snakes in knots.

By the time of my tragic first bow, youngest sister Faiza was already over here with a foster family in Wolverhampton, and Akifa and I were to follow to the United Kingdom shortly after my birth, never to see Juba again. Somehow, I've always felt that my job in life is to make up for all the fuss I've caused from that first appearance, and put out all the positivity into this world I can muster. I like to please people. I'm very much a people person. In fact, nearly all of me is composed of people.

I always put this instinct for wanting to see the best in everyone and everything, and to do all I can to help those so freaked out in desperation as to need my help, down to the genetic influence of my saintly grandpa, The Reverend Jeremiah Wako, who I never got to meet. As for the other half of my DNA, I never had the foggiest, murkiest, most drizzly idea of what was going on, on the XY side. It seems my aunties never knew who my mother was dating, and a brief flurry of introspective inquisition during my pubertal years was met with a traditional whack-based response from Auntie Akifa, as if the Juba family was not enough on its own. But they really are, even given all the catastrophically tragic memories that talk of the past throws up for us.

Mine is not the most rib-tickling origin story, I know. I'm sorry about that, and will try to make up for it, but refugee experiences rarely get them losing sphincter control in the aisles. I open with this to show that as far as I have ever been concerned, I don't have any skeletons in my closet – there might be a few baby teeth in a drawer somewhere, but that's it.

By the few accounts I have, my mother Laila Wako was the middle jewel of three strong sisters, the daughters of a kind-hearted preacher-turned soldier, a widower and, before I was born, yet another sad statistic of the longest civil war in Sudanese history. Laila Wako, they say, was fizzy, and brainy, and beautiful, with a smile like a rainbow arcing from east to west... and all the other things I presume orphans are generally told about their unknown mums.

When Laila died, Akifa, Faiza and little me settled here in the cute market town of Dinham, where the Welsh war zones meet the Black Country vowels, and I grew up in the white-skied Middle-British suburbs.

Trying to get across what it means to live a whole life with no parents is a little like complaining about not having a belly button which dispenses Southern Comfort – I suppose it would have been nice, but we take the breaks with our names on. And I was certainly far from the only kid in school whose father was just a question mark on a government form.

Being born Benjamin Wajih Wako, my name would go through infantile twists and turns as I found my way in this almost entirely rosy-cheeked white neighbourhood. But I do recall the day I announced my solemn decision to rebrand 'Benjy' as 'Banjo'. I was only tiny, and I had clapped eyes and ears on some huge hairy folkie at a summer fete, twanging away on an old clapped-out banjo, and there and then, I sort of fell in love. My Auntie Faiza insists that all I could do for the rest of that day was shout 'BANJO!' and grin.

Since that day, I can't recall a time when Music wasn't my main source of sweetness and light, my soul supper, my, not to put too fine a point on it – essential jam. And words too, not just melody but lyrics – I have a passion for words, the smack and the whoosh and the trickle of them. I unabashedly like to use words like 'unabashedly'.

As Music is my religion, I love too many artists to list, there's barely a genre which doesn't make my veins fizz and pop, from Folk to Funk and back again. But I will always hold true to the first time ever I saw and heard Cab Calloway, that vision in white tux serenading Jake and Elwood Blues with a spine-tingling 'Minnie The Moocher'. It was the first time I recall seeing someone of a similar shade to me really looking *sharp* – white tails, white shoes, white smile, and Black. I think I decided there and then that Cab was who I wanted to be, perhaps with a side order of Freddie Mercury – another beautiful non-white-guy, no matter how very English he seemed in interviews.

The first banjo player I remember jamming with must have been the only Rastafarian redneck in the West Midlands. Another summer fete, and this time a reggae set, personally set up by family friend the good Reverend Bertram Pinker-Byng, to introduce the Rastafari brethren to his little corner of Anglicism. I instantly attempted to become best friends with their banjoist, a huge thickly dreaded bear of a dude called Albert. The band let me play the tambourine, and I eventually had to be dragged away by Auntie Akifa, as they completed packing up.

"Banjo Wako, you are not a Rastafarian, I don't want to hear this 'raas clart' business out of your lips, our ancestors were fighting battles when these lot were smoking hemp, dash it all! Remember, boy – we Wakos have never worn shackles!" This, like so many things, confused little me – there was even racism without white people involved?

The inimitable Saint Cab Calloway it was who nudged me towards sartorial distinction. I am as happy to rock an old t-shirt as the next slob, but if you're setting out to be seen, the collar must be crisp, and the jacket has to be just so. It's a difficult line to walk, especially in a small town like this, as one of the few 'people of colour', as they used to call us, for miles. Dress too decoratively, too flashily, and you're veering on pimphood, inviting the inevitable cries of "Huggy Bear!" But then it's equally dangerous to attempt a look too refined: my attempt to single-handedly bring back the monocle lasted less than one afternoon, after being barraged with lisping Chris Eubank impersonations within five minutes of stepping into the pub. The pale freckly folk round here tend to carry around only so many clichés for Black people, so just being entirely yourself is a constant challenge.

Oh, and then there was that time I thought I'd go 'full Cab', and believed a swish moustache would be just the thing – I walked around with that hanging off my face for at least two months before a close friend kindly took me aside and told me that the face fungus gave me the look of a frightened nark on a witness protection scheme, hiding in the bushes. You see what I mean about lacking a G.A., a reliable guiding voice? Mirrors can be such liars.

Looking back – generally my least favourite direction – my preoccupation with syncopation might have blinkered me a fair bit from the negatives of growing up in such a ghostly white town. There must have come a time when I couldn't ignore that my aunties and I had our own hue positively unique to 1990s Dinham. It almost seemed the town could hold no more than maybe one family of each broad ethnic background, and ideally each was obliged to open a takeaway in the town centre if they wanted to live here.

But if anything, the most tiring attitude in my childhood and beyond was always that well meant but kind of queasy sense of positive discrimination – all those freckly kids with clammy hands wanting to feel how bouncy my 'do was, so many locals wanting to broadcast their hip acceptance of all the children of the rainbow, by sitting next to you on the bus and volunteering a love of Diana Ross. And of course, all the kids in the playground begging me to join them as the only one who could be the Black Power Ranger, or if I was lucky, Winston in 'Ghostbusters'.

There was always Sir Lenny Henry on the TV, bless him, showing us that you could be big and brash and brown and have the whole of Britain giggling on their sofas, but at the same time I couldn't help noticing that Len was having to be a one-man diversity machine, carrying a lot of weight for us all.

The News was often more the place to see folk a little more like us – my Auntie Faiza of course follows the greats like Sir Trevor McDonald and Zeinab Badawi, who's a Sudan girl herself. Or at least, as Auntie Akifa would no doubt snarl, she's a Muslim one, the flavour of religion being of course one of many things requiring the slaughter of millions in Sudan over the centuries, and another reason why it seemed wise for us to get out of the poor old place and over to a milder country, Britain – the big bad Mother who had been meddling with Sudan for so long in the first place.

I don't mean 'guardian angel' literally, obvs. Don't go zooming off down the street with the idea that Theology is any preoccupation of mine, though if I do mention it myself, I was once upon a time the proud winner of a prize novelty rubber for scripture knowledge from Sunday School – it smelt of strawberries, as I recall, and had a cute crucifix on the side. The C of E certainly did us no harm as we settled into Dinham life, and Auntie Akifa became a pillar of the community – stout, cold, stony and round – as the indomitable verger of St Boniface's, stamping ground of the particularly Reverend Pinker-Byng, a dear old duffer with hair and beard like a white cloud, and a face like a blissed-out alpaca.

    The Rev shepherded the parish, took our confirmation classes, and even shoved me in a chorister's dress to try a different kind of music. I still remember the thrill of my first solo performance at St. Boniface's one Midnight Mass, an angel of frills and 'fro – "*Bringing you joy in the morning...*" I sang like the saint I wasn't, and I can almost hear Reverend Bertie now, bleating in his kindly old way, "Yes, yes, bringing joy, my dear chap, joy in the morning, what more can we do in this realm, what?"

    Is it necessary to add that he never fiddled with me? Probably worth spelling out these days. The Rev Bertie was far too, well, Christian in the

12

positive sense for that kind of thing, I'm sure – but you'd have to ask Auntie Akifa. The blessed vicar and she developed what we'll call a close working relationship when I was growing up, and he was a dear old dodo to all of us. He always spoke in this fruity, Lord Snooty, jolly-hockey-sticks-type way which definitely rubbed off on Auntie Akifa, and perhaps me, too. Crikey this, blast and dashed the other.

But, all that said – and though I'd never admit as much to Auntie Akifa for fear of being turned into concrete in twice no time – the good Reverend's influence only went so far, and there came the day when I sneaked off the R.E. exam with my best friend Lotto, a few mushrooms, a huge bottle of cider and a stack of trippy sci-fi DVDs – mainly *Red Dwarf*, as I recall. At the risk of getting a bit too deep, our sudden conception of the infinity of infinity only made us swear an oath, that night, to fill that infinity as best we could with the most music and joy we could muster while we lived. I remained proud of the various Bible-quote-covered prizes I had won at Sunday School, all those smelly rubbers and the like – but Christianity, my bestie and I concluded, was like the ultimate fan club, and one that could get along without us. I do still remember the essentials, though – I think what Jesus was ultimately trying to get across is, 'Don't be That Guy'. You know the one. The really horrible guy.

It was, I've always assumed, Bertie the vicar's influence which bagged our little family two neighbouring flats here at the majestic Wickham Mansions, SY8. The Wickham estate has its detractors, but I love my home. It's a glorious rambling community boasting all manner of life in every corner of its honey-coloured stone edifice, a cloud-scraping menagerie which mushroomed up on the old lower Castle Fields when the late nineties rolled round, new to us just when a growing lad like me needed a bit more room. I actually had two bedrooms, living with both my aunties, whose flats were next door to each other. The Reverend even helped the council turn a blind eye when we dared to knock through, and I developed what in less enlightened times I might have called 'my crib' – a palatial gaff, spa en suite, the works, and always a pleasure to come home to.

These days Auntie Faiza splits her time with her on-off-on again husband Tim in Dudley, so I'm generally lord of the manor. I've always felt the Wicked Wickham Estate was like a grand Muppet Theatre of tasteful theatrical boxes, stretching up several storeys and looming over crumbly lines of Dinham's genuinely antique and weather-worn Georgian houses with what I have always considered to be something of a cheeky wink. All human life is here, and there's very little of that stabbing each other toss which often gets these places a bad name.

It's not all Class As and Prosecco being an H-list – oh, okay, how about Q-list? – celebrity. But I am aware of the reason that some people may still be reading, and I still feel like skirting the obvious business up ahead. But, yes, okay, becoming a one-hit wonder in 2003 was perhaps yet another occasion when I could really have done with a higher power of some sort looking out for me, rather than a dodgy manager called Biffo. I was still scraping along at Dinham School, preparing to flunk my GCSEs when a lazy Music lesson led to a jam which led to the rudimentary Fresh Drones – the hottest boy band of the late summer of 2003 to early spring of 2007.

They do say of the 2000's, "If you can remember being there, then you probably were." I must admit, I was dead against showing up on the *Pop Somebodies* show in the first place – watching that gunk was bad enough, without becoming part of it. The four of us came second on the first series, probably largely due to the abs of my cohorts – certainly, it's no secret that I was the only boy in that boy band with any ability to play or write music. One week we were cringing our way through my early classic, 'Sunny Soul' on national TV, the next thing I knew, contracts were being wafted in front of me, and I signed away my life to the dodgiest pop impresario in a wickedly competitive field. I mean, I would never claim to be the most shrewd spoon in the fork drawer, but push a legal document in front of me and I'm as lost as an asexual in an orgy. "Sign", they said, and they seemed friendly enough, and the pen was very nice indeed, and so I signed. And repented at leisure. It's such an exciting point in any young performer's career, the day they realise they're going to become massively overrated.

I did win one victory, refusing to have the stage name 'Banjo Boiii' (yes, with three i's) forced upon me – an idea I found unacceptable on levels previously unplumbed. At the risk of sounding like scratched vinyl, I repeat that I've always made an effort to present myself as a bloke with a disposition of utmost sunshine, but I do utterly refuse to be anybody's 'boy.' Well, except perhaps my aunties, as they raised me. There was even talk at one point of calling me 'Blue-Eyed Boiii', flagging up the USP of my sparkling blues – a rarity among half-Sudanese dudes, I must admit, and constantly commented upon. But I made my feelings clear.

As for what the contract otherwise dropped me into, it was all beyond me. I do still get something like a quarter of a percent of something or other for writing our only real hit, 'Summer Yet Again' – the soundtrack to a thousand late spring ad breaks – but I rapidly learned that life as a Fresh Drone was not for me. Whatever I threw into that band was thrown away, even the name – and this was long before there were flying machines everywhere called 'drones', I was thinking of bees and Indian music. The fans seemed interested only in my blue eyes and gyrating cohorts, and certainly not the tunes – the only thing I ever cared about.

The truth is, there's a whole wheelbarrow-full of legal reasons why I have to remain vague about this period, none of which I have ever really got, and so it's best to just kick those memories under the rug, then dance all over them. That typed, if the term 'toxic' meant anything at the time besides that song Britney sang wrapped in red plastic, then I would have used it to sum up many of the scenes which went on behind, well, the scenes. It was bad enough having my tunes picked up, watered down and the credit shared five ways, without having to share a tour bus with... ah, now, see, lawyers will sweat, bless the mofos.

Our tour manager, the tremendous Mel Medlicott, did her best with this revolting gang of hormonal post-laddism lads, but I was pretty uncomfortable with how some fans – impressionable ones – were being treated, back in the hotel. And sometimes on the tour bus. Throw a bag of cocaine into a busload of teenage narcissists and just see what happens. I can honestly say the white stuff only ever made me sneeze, so I kept to homegrown pleasures.

In shortest, that just was not in any way my scene, and I had to escape.

There's a certain flavour of slug who would probably whine that this stand was 'virtue-signalling' – a truly dumb concept which only flags up the very real short supply of virtue we are faced with. These vice-signallers are probably the same kind who consider 'Social Justice Warrior' to be a handy term of abuse. I can think of fewer greater things to aspire to, even though I'm not much of a warrior. Perhaps being a Social Justice Jester, or Minstrel, is more my cup of juice.

I'm generally a stranger to high horses, but if the things you really hate in life contain the words 'virtue', 'social justice' and 'correct', think about it: you may as well face facts and start building your own evil underground lair.

All that said, despite being brought up by two intensely strong women – and Auntie Faiza's loud off-camera bellowing about the state of the world must have rubbed off a bit – to say the very least, I have never been remotely political. At any period over the first couple of decades of my life, just ask Banjo Wako about current affairs, and you will have drawn a blank. I can't even keep up with the charts these days. If 'the charts' still exist.

That said, I do recall one wise old voice ringing out when I once accidentally switched on Radio 4, explaining that 'you only have to stand still these days to move to the left'. I knew exactly what that grandpa meant. The worse things out there become, the less any of us can allow ourselves to shrug and suit ourselves – and there's nothing I would naturally like to do more than shrug, shrug, shrug, and have a blissfully chilled time of this short existence.

Any which way but dodgily, even when handed the golden key of groupie paradise, I never felt comfortable treating those on the other side of the gender roundabout as objects. Perhaps being brought up by women has its part to play in this... this... I'm not sure what to call it, this chivalrous instinct. Call it 'white knight syndrome' or whatever colour knight you like. Still just trying to not be That Guy, but to be a gentleman, like my aunties urged me to be.

No matter what my private experiences may have been, using girls like crusty socks never sat well with me, despite it being as good as part of the job description for many rock stars. But I'm not into shallow women who are only interested in your looks, or even worse, what kind of car you drive. (Get knotted, Tracy Chapman.)

Yes, I'll be completely honest here, I have taken part in 'locker room chat': "Hello, have you seen locker 242?" "Sorry, my pound coin has rolled under that bench." "Hope you had a good swim!" and whatnot. Classic

18

stuff. And although it goes against my every ounce to boot a lady's name around, I have had relationships here and occasionally there. It's no secret that there was a period of being dragged around by the far more famous Flora K, Amazonian lead singer of The Skinnybiddies, our *Pop Somebodies* vanquishers. Tall, lissom and apparently utterly incapable of laughing, Flora posters must have been plastered all over a thousand noughties lads' bedroom walls – especially when she became the face (and other bits) of the Eulalie lingerie range – and she now presents one of the *Pop Somebodies* spin-offs, so they tell me.

I may have been the envy of a thousand lairy teenagers, but if you ask me if I felt lucky while Flora and I were an item, it would be unfair to nod. Although of course a stunningly impressive woman in so many ways, back in those days Flora had me trailing along in her wake for months, swearing that she would "make something of me" – presumably some kind of Ikea bedside table. I thought I was doing a pretty good job of making something of myself, i.e. myself. I'm pretty certain, now that I look back, that this affair was some kind of contractual obligation from her point of view, something that worked for her at that time, and she of course dropped me like a radioactive used johnnie as soon as the Fresh Drones' third single stiffed. That was when I felt lucky. And I've never laid eyes on Flora K since – especially not on TV.

Still, as I often say, it's better to have loved and to have lost, than to have loved and to have exploded.

## Chapter Two

So that's it, lovely ladies-stroke-lads – literally, a fresh chapter. If you embarked on this journey with me expecting a tell-all about the Fresh Drones debacle in meaty detail, I hope you kept the receipt, because those are memories I prefer to push away untasted. Those few celeb-ish years were exciting in hundreds of ways, of course, having my own studio flat in Mayfair, zipping around the metropolis on Auntie Faiza'a hand-me-down moped, Trevor, the odd swish dinner at Barribault's, travelling across to New York for failed album launches, the rush of expectation of greatness... but ultimately I felt pigeonholed in the worst way, and I've never been one for pigeons' holes. It wasn't easy or cheap to wriggle my way out of that contract, a straitjacket which kept me running on that wheel of European teen shows, corporate parties and miserable *Pop Somebodies* tours... but I just had to get out, and be myself.

The London years had their moments, of course they did, but I remember limping towards my mid-twenties without any success in all our follow-up releases, the mind-squishing Mayfair rent soon proving far beyond rational, positively pointing me towards homelessness, and above all the feeling of being not so much a has-been as a should-be-but-not-like-this. I asked myself, did I want to stay there in the metropolis at all odds, and live on the streets, in a cardboard box? Did I want to keep trying to be a tiny little fish in a gigantic pond, just another schlepping muso, or instead, to make myself a nice big fish in a far more cosy pond? Or best of all, not any kind of fish at all, and in no kind of pond?

It rattled around my head as I danced around the problem of failing to write another hit: big fish, little fish? Cardboard box?

It seems like everybody these days wants to be a somebody. Personally, I've always wanted to be far more specific. I've never regretted my decision to move back home, and set myself up as – if you'll forgive the sizeable head – a bit of a musical kingpin in the Marches.

At last, I am my own boss. Maybe I should probably go on a staff management course, but I'm nobody's fool. My folly is entirely freelance.

It's not a bad life – the royalties quietly trickle in, making me a self-made thousandaire, and my occasional solo album finds a discerning audience, as do our gigs in the Mark II outfit – The Dinham Drones. You must have heard of us. Surely? I'm also pretty well known around the shires, running open mike nights for years at different pubs, at least a dozen nights a month at £75 a pop, and with festivals and party bookings, I've wasted little lifespan on regrets. It's not as if we're stuck out in a little backwater like Much Middlefold. There's much more to Shropshire than cacky old T'Pau, and Dinham has a music scene to be proud of, especially here at the Angler's – my home from home, a musical Mecca where I'm always proud to perform.

How to describe the ambience of the Angler's to the uninitiated...? It's my heaven, a short stroll to the bottom of the estate and up a short country track, and I'm there, pushing the door open into a world of warmth, light, noise and booze, the exemplary jukebox not drowning out the accompanying whistle of a gourmet scotch egg just missing my 'do as I enter, flung by some dear inebriated friend.

Once known as The Angler's Rest, we get little rest there these days. The riverside pub is not just higgledy but outrageously piggledy, and has been feeding and housing customers for centuries. No doubt Norman knights stood at the bar and complemented the wenches on their pork scratchings. The current management has been here for eons: they have the whole sweep of Yaxley Ales on tap, a dizzying cocktail menu, and best of all, down a rickety old staircase, they have what we call The Love Lounge – my band's home from home.

What our drummer Dobbin (AKA Pete Mulliner) doesn't have at his fingertips in terms of useless muso information isn't worth knowing, just like most of what he does know. But as he would happily tell any unsuspecting virgin to the pub with the lightest provocation, in the heaviest Black Country intonations, "There've been more rock legends propping up that bar than in the whole history of bloody Glastonbury. They've all played here, from, well not The Beatles, obviously, but everyone from the Stones down. Every bugger that matters, that is. Jimi Hendrix puked up something psychedelic in that very booth over there, my Uncle Mo told me. Viv Stanshall lived for a whole month in the gents' toilet back in the mid-seventies. ELO played the Love Lounge before they were even electric, and Jeff had his own beanbag installed. It was right there until just a few years ago, when someone decided to grab it and skite."

I can pretty much transcribe Dobbin monologues word for word after all these years, especially this one: "I know Dinham is hardly Islington," the muso mage likes to say, "and not exactly Beverly Hills, y'know, not quite – but you've got to understand, so many of the greatest stars in Rock Royalty all hung round here in the olden days, and all because they was all mates with – drumroll, obv – 'The Honourable'! You've not heard of 'The Honourable', though? Typical. He was what they call a fixer. In fact, *the* rock and roll fixer. He got things done for all kinds of whacked-out rockers in any spot of bother. And he was from round here, to the manor born. Played on that very piano, round the back, he did. The Hon. is a backstage legend. The myth of myths. A shady figure revered by the wisest musos, and definitely someone surely overdue one of them BBC4 documentaries. When you bring together all the stories, it's bloody weird that people don't know more about the old toff. I mean, what a life – all that celebrity and glamour and then, POOF! He just disappears from the record. Erm, I'll have a double rum and Buck-Up, please, Sonya."

This semi-mythical local celebrity, already forgotten by all but the keenest rock geeks, 'The Honourable', was the son of the local Lord of the Manor – old Lord Yaxley. I was dimly aware of the ancient nob, through my childhood, a crisp white beanpole of a man who occasionally graced the odd church fete and whatnot, though he must have been ninety if he was a minute. His family had some kind of partnership deal with Yaxley

Ales, and we were all particularly grateful to the late Lordship for his agreement to give over a few hundred acres of his vast rolling country estate every June to DIN-DINS: The Dinham Music Festival, running for over 40 years and second only to Glastonbury in the UK music fest stakes. Madonna, Madness, McCartney, who hasn't played Din-Dins? The Dinham Drones have been a mainstay for almost a decade now – we even have our own stage, inherited from a local DJ in the mid-90s who used to run the back room at the Angler's too. Our stage was a kind of circus tent-cum-clubhouse with the desperately dated legend 'ECSTASY' emblazoned all over the hoardings, which was cheesy as frick, but it sort of stuck. 'Ecstasy In The Evening', we call our jam nights. But what's in a name?

We Dinham Drones offer quite a night, not just for the week of the festival in rain or shine, but as the old cry goes – 'weddings, parties, anything'. I should say a little about our line-up, actually, because one thing we agreed when The Dinham Drones was formed was that the old format of lining up on stage and playing to a sea of faces was not just old hat, but crap hat too. And so, all we Drones, like four one-person bands in harmony, we like to play, and to join in the dance.

Dobbin the drummer you know – real name Pete Mulliner, a proper thousandth generation Dinhamian I have already mentioned in all too little detail. Five foot nothing and almost as wide, as part of our stagecraft he has happily given up the traditional drum kit for an incredible sampling kit, strung around his neck, fluorescent sticks aglow as he rips into any rhythm we need. Then there's my technical wizard par excellence and the oldest of my many old friends, of which much more must be said – Lotto Jenkins – on bass and whatever guitar sounds are not provided by our gloriously strutting lothario of a lead guitarist, Neville Badlan – a day-time pig farmer from Shifnal with three kids and *amazing* hair. And of course, there's me, on vocals, and my wonderful unique breed of heavily customised rosewood-bedecked keytar, name of Minnie: a wonder of sonic engineering with mahogany finish, a kitsch '80s original expertly pulled apart and put back together again by my right-hand human Lotto, which is capable of emitting positively any sound discernible to human ear.

Besides our own music – at last performed on my own terms – we'll happily attempt any old cover you fancy. We earn our crusts by our music and we live to please, be it 'Bohemian Rhapsody', 'Baby Got Back' or 'Barbie Girl', if we know it – and Dobbin knows every song ever sung – we do it. And the crowds, it would be dense to deny it, do love it, mingling with the music as the lights bedazzle and the perspiration pours. The energy that we four can create to order in any sweaty venue you like has become in hot demand the whole West Midlands over, if not Wiltshire.

"If music be the food of love", we say, "squirt some sauce on it." I'm very proud, in fact it's what I have always lived for, spreading that joy around a hot banging room, in amongst the dancers and the singers and the yellers and the partygoers, all sharing in that joy we bring with our tunes. I'm the least spiritual person you will ever meet, but sometimes it is almost a spiritual thing. There's a lot to be said for joy in the morning, but give me ecstasy in the evening every time.

## Chapter Three

I'm no expert on all this just yet, obvs, but talk of Din-Dins does suggest a new chapter. Perhaps that's where this spine-jangling story really begins, a year or three ago, on a hot June afternoon.

Festival season is what it's all about, really, for those of us who have devoted our lives to music and showing off generally. The once-green lower slopes of the Yaxley estate were glowing golden in the sunshine, flags and decorations of all conceivable colours and patterns flapped in the breeze, and the aromas of all kinds of exotic foods filtered out of the many exotic street food stalls, and mingled with the gentle aroma of frying poo to create that cocktail of smells which truly defines the best summer rock festivals.

At that time, I had been tentatively seeing a fair bit of Poppy Pirbright. She had proudly reclaimed the fascistic derogatory term 'manic pixie dream girl', arguing that she was happy to lay claim to being all of those things, depending on mood.

And now, having taken up so much expanse of long-dead tree protesting my deep-rooted respect for the traditional less beardy side of the gender spectrum, I have to fall back on a big splash of outdated objectification, as Poppy is generally regarded in the shire as one of those girls who just can't help it – 'it' being triggering the eyeballs of discerning witnesses of all discerning genders (and quite a few species) to pop out on stalks. Real cartoon wolf catnip. Green eyes right out of any lonely RPG video game developer's action heroine design folder, with cascades of luscious hair naturally in the most vivid shade of red, sometimes layered with black and turquoise. Poppy is a willowy firework whom less enlightened generations could well have defined as 'hot stuff' or maybe a 'peach' or a 'pippin' in every aesthetic sense. Great fun at parties too.

But – and believe me, my every atom clenches at the need to add this – Poppy is sometimes, how can I put it? Expert Level. I mean, how would you feel if you were presented with this positively Venusian assembly of fragrant curves and dimples, and then asked by them out of a clear blue sky whether you truly believed that 911 was staged by George Bush, or, like her, Prince Philip? Or to be fervently informed by them in exasperated tones that chem-trails in the sky are the poison that blinds so many of us to the antics of an invisible faerie race, who are always zipping around the place meddling in human affairs? Keeping an open mind is important in life, I know, but I've always felt it's equally wise not to keep your mind so open that it flaps about all over the place and gets covered in crap. Even the most open minds need to have some kind of security system to prevent fly-tipping. Poppy's mind was clearly absolutely larded with dangerous tosh, with everything from the existence of 'lovely little flying frog people who I have definitely seen dancing around by the bins behind the One Stop shop' to 'the absolute impossibility of humans ever reaching the Moon, no matter what the lying media tell you' liable to plop out of her undeniably tulip-turned and somewhat hypnotising lips at any given time.

There was a season where she seemed to have picked me out as a personal sparring partner, and it would have been rude to say no. She had spelled out in words of one syllable that I was more than welcome to behave as badly as I wanted with her, but that sheer level of gullibility was such a profound turn-off, taking any kind of advantage of P.P. seemed tantamount to seducing a flowering cactus.

We finally parted whatever brass rags we had when she instigated a loud argument about the existence of Shakespeare, who she seemed to believe was a fictional character. Now, I don't claim to be the biggest expert on old baldie Bill, but there was a dude who knew words aplenty. Though nobody would dub me a scholar, I've enjoyed some of the man's films, and ever since one school trip to Stratford, I always felt a certain pride in the greatest poet in history being a sort of local fellow artiste. West Midlands represent and all that.

"Squeegee your fourth eye, dude!" Poppy steamed, "You really do just fall for anything the MSM want you to believe, Banjo, you poor boy. Such a shame you're so hot, you can't seem to make that mental jump to see the truth, that Shakespeare never even existed! That's just fact. It was in a movie, you really should have seen it."

"Okay... so all those poems and plays and..."

"Oh, Banjo", she simmered. "All Shakespeare's books were written by Elizabeth the first – you know the one, the ginger, the first trans King of England."

"Yes, well... perhaps I should have seen that film, yes. Which is your favourite?"

"Favourite what? King?"

"No, Shakespeare play."

"Well I haven't read any of them obviously. Why would I when they're fakes? I have seen *The Lion King* though."

"Was that by Elizabeth the first too?"

"Bahaha-ho, you are a feather-head, Banjo", she chuckled in reply, tousling my carefully coiffured bonce.

I soon learned to engage with Poppy as little as possible when these moments of conspiracy codswallop flared up. Perhaps connected to her, let's say individual grasp of reality, was Poppy's constant thirst for chemical stimulation. I've never been one for the pills and powders myself, the music brings most of the pleasure for me, perhaps the odd J once the day's entertainment is complete, as my sole herbal reward. Occasionally beforehand too. And at other times, yes. But just as she was always happy to cram any quarter-baked conspiracy into her brain, Poppy would happily snort a line of fire ants if you told her they altered your perception for half a millisecond, and yah-boo-sucks to the consequences.

Returning to this Din-Dins, shortly before I finally managed to convince Poppy to end our brief 'special friendship' – largely by my inability to consummate it, though again, this was a time when a helpful advisor would have been welcome. We were enjoying the sunny pleasures of Din-Dins, a few hours before the D.D.'s Ecstasy In The Evening set began, and having introduced a guest band who had a whole hour's slot, mainly doing Hall & Oates covers as I recall, I was free to wander off for a wander. Poppy came with me, and it's hard to say what substance, what herb or what insect she had been ingesting, but she was in one of her particularly fizzy moods, the kind of mood which inspires the strongest of men to stand well back and try to merge tastefully into the wallpaper.

We were strolling arm in arm along the gravel paths where once England's most in-bred elite must have strolled with their damsels, when we spied Circular Sam – AKA Pretend Police Constable Sam Blount. 'Circular' is not a kind nickname, I know, some of this world's sweetest occupants sit firmly on the chubby side of the spectrum. Dear Dobbin, for one-plus, is proudly stout, being built on the Toby Jug assembly line, but he makes it work gloriously for him. And this Sam wasn't quite so circular in our schooldays, when he was a bully fond of knocking every shade of shit in the rainbow out of any kid even vaguely inclined to be interesting. So he didn't exactly make it easy to feel sympathetic either then or now, and it was little surprise when he achieved his life's ambition of wearing the shiny tit of the local constabulary for a living – or at least, as a Police Community Support Officer, a stomping bauble of fluorescent malevolence, largely responsible for reporting missing recycling bags and dealing with the odd escaped sheep.

On the day in question, Sam was ambling along in the usual hi-vis vest, sporting a new and notably sickly attempt at a moustache, positively leaving a trail of sweat in his wake like a particularly officious snail.

I've been lax in failing to introduce a singular character into the proceedings here – Homer, Poppy Pirbright's frightening familiar, and presumably the result of a horrifically passionate affair between a pitbull terrier prone to chewing on the bitterest of wasps and loving it, and a toxic chihuahua. The brute made even Auntie Akifa's Apple seem kind-hearted, and I still bear the imprint of that little antichrist's teeth in my right calf.

PCSO Blount eyed the grizzling four-legger with a mixture of fear and undying hatred.

"That dog o' yours behavin' itself, Poppy?" he puffed. "Should be on a lead in a place like this, him's a menace."

"How dare you threaten my darling Homer with your barbaric and sick tools of BDSM punishment?" Poppy fired back, with more nettle than I would have dared.

"I's only doing my duty, madam", the stout PCSO replied, officiously, levering off his checkered cap as he sponged the ooze off his broad brow. "It's all well and good you lot having your druggy fun here on the estate, but someone has to police that fun."

"Well, go and police it somewhere else, and stop oppressing innocent doggy-wogs."

Some kind of small internal flame seemed to flicker in Blount, and after a moment's pause, he turned to me. "Banjo. You carrying, then?"

"My dear Sam," I replied, "I thought you knew me better than that. I have about as much interest in chemical substances as you have in..." I had been on the verge of saying 'calorie control', but managed to stop myself in time – not being That Guy. "... erm, in the plays of Elizabeth the first", I hastily swerved.

"Aah, well, just you be careful, don't forget I'd be well within my rights to search you in every crook and nanny, inside and out, if my suspicions be strong enough", he huffed. "I know what you lot are like, you... you *entertainer*."

I was slightly taken aback. I had never seen the circular copper before me as any kind of bosom buddy, but was he really threatening to caution a person of colour, on his most hallowed turf, with a gig only a couple of hours away?

"Has anyone ever told you that you're a dazzlingly handsome man, PCSO Blount?" I asked.

Whatever brain lay beneath his cap seemed to take a dramatic tumble, another sting of fear flashed into his eyes, and all he could do was stammer: "... N-no."

"No, I thought not," I replied. "You'll excuse my little jest, I couldn't help it, you know, being one of those *entertainers*. But when you're right, you're right. I'm telling you just in case you ever are."

His swine-like eyes narrowed, and he had the gall to prod a sticky finger at my rather natty lavender collar. "Just you watch it, I've got both my eyes on both of you... Banjo."

I swore he was a beat away from ending with 'Boy'. I gave him full force of my least sincere smile, and he turned to amble away.

Just then an event long in the brew finally seemed to bubble over, with several things happening at once. Homer, who had been growling throughout the proceedings and eying Sam with the burning righteous hatred of someone who had caught their local Tory MP assaulting their baby, and at the sight of the special constable's especially vast behind, all his canine instincts became impossible to contain, even with his mistress there to keep him in check, and with a howl and a bark, he set off after the cop with the vim of the hungriest of hunters.

I'd never have credited PCSO Blount with athletic prowess, but with the quickest glance back, he streaked off in flight from the animal with the squeakiest squeal, parting the crowds at an MPH which had to be seen to be believed, his policeman's cap tumbling to the floor behind him.

Poppy laughed fit to burst, and it was the work of a millisecond for her to pick up the hat and place it on her head, dancing around the festival with it on at a rakish angle.

It must have been the best part of an hour later, with The Dinham Drones gathered in the Ecstasy tent and our next set all-but imminent, that PCSO Blount was again spied from afar, on the hunt for his missing headgear.

I turned to Poppy. "Now, it goes without saying, Poppy, that you *are* carrying all sorts of dodgy substances, no?"

She gave me a blazing grin, though her eyes seemed to be fixed on the horizon. And in a flash, I took the black checkered cap off her head and tried to find somewhere safe to stash it. She may have been so annoying as to make my mind swim, but it wouldn't do to see her dragged away to the cells in Leominster. It must have been a few seconds after I took charge of the helmet that Blount looked in our direction, and came storming over.

"Stealing policeman's hats is a very serious offence, Wako", he thundered.

"What about wanky special constable's hats?" Poppy began, but I had to silence her.

"Look, Sammy," I began, "I merely found this Village People costume piece on the floor here, and was trying my very best to track the owner down and restore it to them."

"A likely story!"

"Thank you. Very glad to be the hero of the hour, preventing your poor shiny bonce from being roasted into a sizzling gammon."

"I think you'd better–"

And then a new voice speared through the muggy atmosphere, and the closest earthly thing to any G.A. or H.P. stalked forwards.

"PCSO Blount, if you find yourself even dreaming of wrongfully detaining the Talent who is about to marshal the next three hours of entertainment on this hallowed stage because of a bit of festival tomfoolery, I am intimately familiar with precisely the right people to tweak, to ensure that your uniform goes back in its dressing-up box for good. Kindly police the populace elsewhere."

Yes, life without Mrs. J would have been a far more problematic mess, it must be shouted loud. The landlady of the Angler's was a Samson upon whom the whole edifice of Dinham often seemed to rest, a woman the word 'handsome' had been created for, a clear head taller than me, with silvery quiff and effortless grace. Her long limbs and warm manner gave her the appearance of a female praying mantis who could easily chomp your head off for a quick snack, but is perfectly happy to let you scuttle away.

Not just landlady and beloved festival organiser, she was and gloriously remains CEO of Yaxley Ales – co-owned with the Yaxley Estate – and indeed of Buck-Up, the all-natural energy drink whose production employs at least half of the Dinham population. I know this fizzy dayglo gunk needs no introduction, the stuff is guzzled by knackered consumers from Mumbai to the Mumbles and back, in flavours from Lychee to Spam, and I have been known to knock back the odd Elderflower Buck-Up to add oomph to a late-night gig.

And of course, as she hinted, Mrs. J has many old friends up at the Castle. Nothing was more likely to cow the pig than bringing out the big nobs, and so off Blount slunk, with a bitter warning to Poppy to "Watch out for your doggy – wog!" as he slank.

And so, my good name restored, we Dinham Drones were free to cajole a horde of chilling festival-fairies to roll where the aisles would have been had they been there. You just imagine Queen at Knebworth… and so will I.

This was the solitary slug in the glorious fresh salad dished up by Din-Dins that year, and I was just propping up the bar at the Angler's one evening, discussing the plans for the first Din-Dins of this new decade with the boss over a pint of Yaxley Gold when the first sniff of something truly rotten reached our nostrils.

"Ooh looks like it's time o'clock!" my drummer Dobbin announced, downing his pint and ordering another in one swift movement. The other Drones, as was their wont, were heatedly debating which Muppet would play which member of a 90s Britpop band.

"You cloth-brained knob, Louise Wener is clearly far more of a Janice than a Miss Piggy!" Lotto was hollering.

"So says the woman – sorry, girl, I means, dude – who reckons Kermit would make a better Damon Albarn than Liam Gallagher!" cried Neville.

"Look," Dobbin mediated, "At least we've agreed that Scooter is Jarvis."

"'At's indubitable, shag."

Some people say we should do a Dinham Drones podcast, but instead we just go to public spaces and talk too loudly about stuff.

Mrs. J managed to cut through this guff without raising her voice one decibel: "Banjo, my dear man, chief of the imponderables which arise from utilising 'Horror' as a theme for your stage is that it will turn the proceedings into a frankly incongruous Hallowe'en party, four months premature."

"Yes, I see that, but I've found this absolutely stunning lounge suit fit only for the full Dracula works, Mrs. J, and I just thought that this year..."

"Forgive me, sshh," she held up one spade-like, ring-glittering hand. "Your aunt is on the television."

The gigantic TV which filled the back wall of the bar was always tuned to catch the evening *Midlands This Evening* airing at this time, and I had always felt a pang of pride at the instinctive hush which settled for any report from neighbourhood TV star, Faiza Malone.

"It's an exclusive so out-of-the-blue Twitter hasn't even had a sniff of it, but an hour or so ago the Hurl Corporation released the news that its CEO, Troy Van Hurl, the business magnate and controversial Tweeter, was resigning to accept the inheritance of the Earldom of Yaxley, the ancient British estate based in Yaxley Castle, in South Shropshire.'

A drone shot zooming over the crumbly old pile filled the screen, as Auntie Faiza continued. "The Yaxley Estate – co-owner of Yaxley Ales, making it one of the few profitable aristocratic families left in the UK, has been in limbo since the death of the 16th Earl in 2018. I spoke to the late Earl's sisters, Lady Roberta Mannering-Phipps-Epstein and Lady Angela Mannering-Phipps-Little.'

"Roll out the double barrels!" I began to sing, but was shushed.

There appeared on screen two almost identical old birds standing outside the Castle, one in a kaftan of all imaginable colours, the other only

38

a wimple short of full nun outfit. I'd certainly seen them around town over the years, but had always assumed it was one old lady with massive mood swings.

The grey lady spoke first: "Our family can be traced back at least to the glorious conquest of King William, you know, and the Baron de Mainwaring."

"Or was it Phippeys?"

"No, it was Main-Waring. When our dear second brother passed away without issue, I'm afraid the ancient rules of our lineage forbade either of us from assuming any formal role."

"It's all men, darlings," the rainbow lady chimed in, as if nobody else had spoken. "Nobody but males of the bloodline can inherit, a stupid oath taken by men centuries ago. Both Bill and dear Daddy, as the Earl, could have shaken things up a bit, but they just never seemed to get round to it. We both have daughters, you see. It's all so terribly toxic. And now here we are."

"There's nothing wrong with men, Bobbie."

"Darling – there's something wrong with everybody."

Auntie Faiza purred, to numerous gross archive clips: "*And now here we are*': with the prosperous Earldom and vast Yaxley Estate in the heart of the Welsh Marches – home, of course, to the annual Din-Dins rock festival – poised for a takeover by one of Wall Street's most outspoken wolves.'

His great big yellow head filled the screen, teeth sparkling like tin foil in the trash.

"Oh yeah, I'm very proud to be British, why not?" Hurl beamed from the steps of his Manhattan offices. "Raised on Wall Street, born in Johannesburg, we all know that, I don't deny it. As you know, if I had been born right here there would be a different ass in the Oval Office right now. But I visited that place, that England Castle, many times growing up, and sure, my blood is as blue as it gets. Heheh. It's just a fact, you know? It's all in the blood."

"That bloke's got a knob like a fly's eyelash," Dobbin correctly observed. "He's got so much sand up his vagina he could give donkey rides."

Another interview, a stark blue studio with 'FOX' blaring all over it. "As you know, I never knew my fathers," the mound of dayglo dung's lip jutted out, followed by a nodder from some kindly Aryan lady. "I was just a baby, just me and my mother, and then I got adopted by so many men over the years, but I'm a self-made man, you know, everyone knows this, but I'm a proud Mannering-Phipps, so it has become clear to me."

Auntie Faiza's voice blessedly drowns him out: "The self-crowned King of Twitter flamings has faced criticism in the past for his political ambitions, and association with groups including far-right British organisation The White Knights of the United Kingdom, led by fellow controversialist and so-called 'truth activist' John Bull, real name Simon Ludlow-Starkey."

If any image could be more hideous than Hurl's face, it was the next rushed montage of straggling clumps of red-faced gammon, roaring in the streets, throwing bottles, all tattooed, beflagged or otherwise adorned

40

with their double-white logo, a kind of St. George cross, but white-crossed on white, quite a triumph of the worst kind of stupidity. Then back to that face. A face which truly made any sane person alter their whole conception of Humanity as Evolution's last word.

"Ya know, I like being tan! A good, golden tan, man," the old zit popped, "But above all I like being white. I am a golden example of the Anglo-Saxon race, and I'm very, very happy with that, ya know? We own the world. Am I a racist because I say I'm proud of that? So I have been having meetings with some very good people... Rich white male privilege is a complete myth, and anyone who says otherwise won't bother me, because of... three secret reasons."

Back to the New York streets. "But I am not a White Knight, I'm way better than that now! I'm gonna be in the House of Lords, baby!"

"Will you be relocating to Yaxley Castle, Mr Hurl?" called out some unseen interested party.

"Hey, that's your highness now, buddy! Yeah, I got a few things to tie up here, my son and daughter gotta be trained to take the reins, you know, and then we'll take up our new affairs of state, you know, The Duke of Earl Yaxley. I'm not sure I wanna live in an old castle, though. Dungeons I like, you can do a lot with a good dungeon, but from what people are saying to me, it sounds like that place has been just crawling with hippies for a long time. But I hear they really need a good golf course out there." And he grinned, right to camera.

"It looks like a breath of fresh air for the British nobility, but how that breath will smell, nobody yet knows. Faiza Malone, Yaxley Castle, Shropshire," for Midlands This Evening .'

"And now the spor–"

The screen went dead. Mrs. J brandished the remote control. Those who know her well all swear that one of her eyebrows flickered.

"Indeed?" she said.

## Chapter Four

After that slug to the sacs, for all the regulars watching, things understandably took a turn for the oblivious. Mrs. J absented herself stiffly, tipping a wink for her deputy, barkeep pride of Dinham Sonya Postlethwaite, to extend the extensive tabs for me, Lotto, Dobbin and Neville – at least for as long as Neville dared stay out, with kids to scrub and feed and whatnot. Joint sorrows, drowned in oceans of booze, led to a lock-in of truly Rolling Stone proportions, barely a bellow of which I can remember.

But I can certainly recall the abominable rude awakening the next morning. Wrenched from the numbness of sweet deep kip, sudden paralysing hangover struck me, and so I began to patiently remind myself that I surely had no soul for Satan himself to have used as a toilet, as seemed to be the case. I was still trying to work out how to evict the family of exploding walruses who had apparently taken up residence in my poor sensitive head, when a familiar roar blasted through the letterbox, into my aching consciousness.

"BANJO, YOU LIFELESS YOUNG REPROBATE, YOU!" the entirety of the Wickham Estate rang, "WHERE ARE YA, YOU WANT AN AUNTIE'S CURSE LAID UPON YOUR SHORT AND SHAGGIES?"

I glanced at the clock. Half-past eight. I had forgotten there was a half-past eight. What I desperately needed was some kind of ultimate pick-me-up, a life-saver of a potion, but what I got, was an auntie apocalypse.

It had been many a morning since *Midlands This Evening*'s finest had last come stomping around her old crib – generally she shared a palatial place in Dudley with her husband, Tim Malone, and daughter, my cousin Viv. Back in the early '90s Belfast boy Tim had been a teenage chief tea-maker to his namesake Sir Thingy-Lee just about the time that he pulled the lever to unleash the World Wide Web on the planet. As a result the temp made good, gaining ground-floor entrance to a whole ton of Dot-Com businesses, where he fiddled with logos and suchlike, before having the good fortune to pull out of all of them before the Millennium, when they were still worth millions, and not penny-chews. The problem is, he's used his wealth to retire early and become an avid collector of geeky memorabilia, with row upon row of black-eyed, bulbous-headed dolls filling every wall, and he often allows his geeky tendencies to get the better of him, turning over as much of the homestead as he dares into his own personal Batcave of allegedly priceless collectibles. As in, he has literally carved out a Batcave in their basement – and this can sometimes cause a tremor in the happy family foundations, sometimes requiring Faiza to spend a few days back in our flat, to calm down. She stayed a whole fortnight when he unveiled the Starship Enterprise deck in their attic.

But it usually takes something big to bring her back home in this way – not least as it means giving up Viv's cooking. That girl will make a

44

world-class chef one day, I often try to cadge an invitation to the geek museum when she's doing her *Goraasa be dama with Ful Medames*.

And so, despite the desolate war zone which was my cranium on this morning, I expressed concern as I slugged over to click on the kettle.

"My dear, lovely, wonderful auntie of my bosom," I croaked, "You find me in the last stages of deathly poison, but what brings you home?"

"To my own flat?"

"To our home, dear auntie."

"I know that look. You look like you've been drinking Dinham to the dregs again."

"We may have had... a huge amount, yes."

"Haha, that's my boy."

"And actually, auntie, you started it!"

"WHAT?"

A galaxy-blasting boom. I cringed. "Never mind. I hope no storm clouds have formed over Malone-land? You're not here for a holiday from the Geekatorium?"

"No, love – your Uncle Tim's on cloud ninety-nine right now – he just nabbed a pair of the actual kecks Alec Guinness wore in *Star Wars* for a knock-down price!" she roared, and my brain pulsated. "Jonathan Ross was crying!"

I was just pouring a slosh of hot water into a cup full of coffee granules when she approached from behind and wrapped me in an embrace which would have earned a caution for severity from a particularly needy boa constrictor. "And besides, why do I need any special reason to come and see my ugliest nephew?"

"Your only nephew!" I exhaled, sure that my poor brain was now a cert to come squirting out of my nostrils.

"And the smartest!" she beamed. "Earl Grey for me, ta! No, I took the chance to pop over to the shire because there was word in the newsroom of some kind of dodgy dancey drug doing the rounds in Dinham. You haven't heard anything about it?"

"My dear Faiza," I responded, thankfully somewhat re-humanised by the first half-pint of feel-better-juice, and tying the cord around my dressing gown with more pique than I could have mustered moments before. "As you know, I would never touch a crystal, flake, pill or grain of illicit substance any dodgier than the most natural herb you can find growing in the attic of any of Shropshire's finest. Or, for that matter, the legal stuff brewed round the back of the Angler's."

"Yes, I know, you're a good boy when you want to be – oh, and can you roll a little one for me to have later, thanks? But you do know *everybody*, Banjo, the police are no good, so who am I going to turn to but musicians? No problem anyway, it's no story. What I'm really here for is to gift you with an absolutely bostin' little job."

"Would this be as little a job as the time you sent me all the way to California to pick up what Uncle Tim insisted was the one and only prototype of the IronCow special Silver edition vinyl doll and pencil case, with orders to haggle over the price, only to find myself hauled up by the LAPD for handling a stolen cow?"

A dark chapter, this, and another time my so-called guardian angel had been caught playing pocket pool on the job. As I have some musical buddies in LA they had kindly arranged a few solo gigs over there – American tips for performers being twice the average fee over here – and Uncle Tim happened to mention what a favour it would be if I could liaise with the seller over this apparently hugely rare toy. You know me – anything for a pal, but once again, I found myself toying with absolute disaster and several years wearing an impossible orange jumpsuit. I only managed to get back to the airport and home because the cops were so confused to meet a man of my colour with an accent like this, they resisted the urge to taser the solids out of me, and ordered me to leg it. Verbosity can be a handy weapon in Los Angeles.

Well, there was that, plus the luck of one Officer Dwayne Balowski being such a major fan of the classic cartoon series *IronCow Vs Baby Blobbs* – the endless clashes between a crime-fighting millionaire cow and a crime-boss toddler, this one good apple could see in a second that it had to be the seller who was guilty of flogging fake memorabilia to gullible Irishmen with far more money than sense, and I had no case to answer. I even kept the fake IronCow pencil case: a funny little thing, silvery plush with red flashing lights, catchphrase samples and a fat zipper down the udders.

Auntie Faiza broke out into a laugh which easily circumvented any caffeinated calm in my war-torn innards, and chucked my cheek, uninvited. "Bless you, love, are you still going on about that? No, this is a fun job, you and your little dinmakers'll be knocked bandy!"

I raised an eyebrow to just the edge of agony.

"It's a gig, Banjo – a big 'un, too! I've managed to get your band the wedding reception for Terry Scholfield's fourth wedding, and here's the kicker – it's at the Castle!"

"Yaxley Castle?" I gaped.

"No, bloody Castle Grayskull! Of course Yaxley, up at the big house! It'll be proper lush, and he's paying top whack. Apparently he gets the place for free because he was the nephew of the old Earl or something."

This was a lot to dump on a dude with a melting brain. It would certainly be a high profile do for the Drones. Telly Terry, the grinning veteran anchor of *Midlands This Evening,* already had three wives behind him when he suddenly made a hugely publicised proposal to his boyfriend Lionel live on air. A local spot for Children In Need, I think. So it was a cert to be that year's ultimate celebrity reception. Who wouldn't want that gig? Maybe me.

"But auntie, the show we put on is loud, and hot, and sweaty, I'm really not sure the Dinham Drones are a Yaxley Castle kind of outfit."

"Bollocks, Banjo, you lot are always playing those ancient tunes from an 'undred years ago, put on your nattiest togs and give 'em a bit of that, you know..." She began some stodgy-limbed send-up of the Charleston, and stole my toast.

The blessed pantheon of Calloway, Holliday and co aside, do you recall the nineties success of a little single called 'Doop'? Ironic 'twenties' jazzamaniac throwback stuff. I loved it, and fresh beats with flapper sensibilities remain a speciality to this day. In fact, an old pile like Yaxley couldn't be a better venue for us to have our 21st century tributes to the hits of the jazz era belt out – those crafty white thieves Kern, Gershwin, Porter, Berlin... But then, the horror began leaking out of my chopped liver brain, the disaster which we had been drinking to forget...

"Hey up, hang on, I'm not playing any gig in the home of Troy bastardising Van Hurl, spit!"

She quite rightly let out a grunt of distaste. "Ugh, no. Don't you worry about that, this was all agreed before he dropped his bloody bombshell. You were watching last night, then?"

I nodded my head, and the universe lurched. "You don't think he was serious about the golf club thing?"

"Christ knows what 'serious' means to him, me old darling. When I started out in the news lark, the ones with all the power could be boring, or cruel, or bigoted, but they were at least capable of being serious. When you needed to be, you know? These days, you may have noticed, all power goes to those who are best able to troll the maximum rightful thinking citizens. I reckon that if the likes of him have ruined as many days as possible, every day, that's probably enough for him."

"But surely Troy is rich enough already?"

"Don't call him Troy, his name is 'Mr Van Hurl' at best – or actually, it turns out, 'Mr Mannering-Phipps-Van-Hurl, Earl of bloody Yaxley.' Getting everyone to use his first name is all part of the game, humanising a subhuman slob. And there's no such thing as 'rich enough' for him – it's not even his own money, he inherited it from his daddy when he was a baby, and he's been losing it ever since. They want me to interview the orange scrote when he gets here. I'm trying to decide if it's something I can physically do without raking my nails down his raggedy neck."

It has often been said of my auntie, off-camera, that she is *never* outraged, but always has an extra bit of rage to get out. It would be surprising that she still had her job, given the volume of her outbursts, if she wasn't so damn good at it. "Oops, pardon me, and  my lack of editorial 'balance'," she laughed, slapping her own wrist, "Balance? Between a rich racist rapist and would-be fascist, and basic decency! But don't worry, the party's at the weekend, he won't be there by then."

"Well that is something..." I ummed and nearly erred, until Auntie Faiza's smile shrank.

"You'm doing the gig, Banjo. I had to pull several strings and fiddle with at least one gromit to get my nephew the society wedding of the season! You'll enjoy it."

As ever with my dear auntie, I realised this was more a direct order than a reassurance. I rolled her the requested J, she mussed up my undeniably gigantic bedhead bush, and passed through to have a moan with her big sister, who was already hunched up in her usual chair, strangling Apple and watching the racing from Aintree.

"Banjo!" Auntie Akifa barked, once Faiza had left. "You're playing your abominable beat music at the big house?"

"It very much looks like it, auntie, yes."

"Standards must be dropping, then," she growled. "That place will be crawling with those blasted bum-men I told you about, you know that, you take good care of your tuppence, boy."

Now, Auntie Akifa had brought me up, I owed her the eternal patience of any orphan kept securely out of the care system, and that patience generally involved biting my lip so often when she hit a seam of her own brand of bigotry that it should by rights resemble a cornish pasty. You'd hope that the things she'd had to put up with since coming to Britain would have inspired some degree of empathy, but no, it's still "Hell-sent Polish Romanians" and "devilish bum burglars".

I comfort myself with the legend of Auntie Akifa's run-in with racism back when I was a schoolboy. She opened the door to our flat to discover some rotten little thug – it may even have been Sam Blount, judging by her description of "Big fat ugly bad-lad skinhead" – with a mysterious brown paper bag, apparently about to post it into our sweet-smelling home.

"What do you have there, boy?" she asked, cold as a pint of liquid nitrogen.

"Um... chocolate mousse!" the lad apparently replied, a rabbit caught in the headlights of the Akifa juggernaut.

"In a bag? Well, why don't you go ahead and enjoy some of that mousse, young man?" She hissed back... and the story goes that he did. He stood there and shovelled that brown stuff into his gob under Akifa's fiery eye, and probably enjoyed it, before she let him go.

All that said, on this occasion, still a-quiver as I was, Akifa's usual paranoia about my indoctrination into the horrors of man-love did trigger a mild "Jeez..." to escape my lips.

"Banjo, kindly do not swear at your auntie who brought you up with all the love of the Lord! Don't speak his name with your dirty mouth in that way." Her lips pursed like the bumhole of a particularly nervous cat. "You boys can make your noise in a castle all you like, but it'll never be a proper job, Benjamin Wako. Who knows though, maybe if you do keep away from all them bad men you might find yourself a nice girl there at last. I say, a man of your age should be up and married, boy! Where are my blessed grand-nieces and nephews? There's this lovely accountant who plays the piano at the Sunday school, Adele Pimworthy, she does pong a bit, but she's surely still fertile. DO something with your life!" And having reached poison plateau, she returned to the gee-gees, clutching her betting slips close to her cardy. And Apple's eyes returned to their sockets.

Trying to match me with sundry unsuitable churchgoers was one of Auntie Akifa's favourite forms of torture. Few days go by without some mention of my three-day engagement to one transient member of the St.

Boniface's flock, PE teacher, Hortensia Lubbock, a well-built and striking woman who would give your average Amazonian an inferiority complex. Though no half-pint myself, half a week of being dandled around by Hortensia like an under-inflated sex doll had resulted in an allergy to her righteous healthiness only solved by my going on a week-long bender of gin, weed, cake and blasting out Satanic Metal which inspired her to blessedly pop the pin in the whole affair. I was glad at least to have avoided any mention this time. I paused.

"Thank you, Auntie Akifa, yes, I will. I will do all of that. Nephews and nieces coming right up. Just as soon as we've played this wedding reception. Come on Apple," I added, with maximum dignity, "Walkies."

## Chapter Five

It was odd to think that I hadn't actually set foot inside Yaxley Castle since
a rare tour as part of a garden party back when I was an infant. I do
remember some old tall dark johnnie leading us sprogs around like
ducklings, pointing out the rusty old suits of armour and so forth, but ever
since, it never seemed the kind of place you would ever actually go into.
The old pile always provided nothing less than a majestic background to
the madness of the Din-Dins festival, basking in the summer sunshine, all
crumbly towers and honey ruins, an icon of the British summer, but to me
– a mystery.

Nonetheless, dressed in my third-finest, I was pleased to find myself
far from cowed by the pong of centuries of aristocratic privilege as Lotto
and I arrived for an agreed recce of the venue in the chilly late winter
dusk. I'd say we were both in pretty good shape – roughly humanoid – but
there was some huffing and puffing when we arrived, as the castle was the
best part of a mile uphill. The real best part of the mile being the top bit.

"Hang on, Banjo, are we supposed to look for a tradesman's entrance?"
Lotto wondered.

"My dear dude, you are talking to the winner of a 2003 ITV pop star
contest, I don't do tradesmen's entrances", I said, and reached for the big
brass bell-ringing-thing. A distant jangling could be heard, and years of
costume dramas suggested some kind of lurching butler in a penguin suit
would soon be trudging up to open the door.

Instead, after some time and much unlocking, a tiny person boasting a passing resemblance to a budgerigar which had fallen into a cup of hot tea shot his face out with what seemed like aggressive intent.

"Who's this now? Oh, it's you, Ben-German."

Little Pat Pirbright – essentially Mr. Potato Head, but considerably less brown, always pronounced my name like that, and he always struck me as perversely opposite to his daughter Poppy, height aside, on the few occasions when I found myself in 'extremely hypothetical father-in-law' situations with him. His bristly moustache bristled further, and he cast his Tory gaze up at our towering heights.

"Mr. Pirbright!" I found myself bowing. "I didn't know you had become a butler?"

"I'll buttle you in a minute, you cheeky young get. There's been no butler at the castle for decades, we're here cleaning! My mother, she was Head Parlour Maid here back in the 50's. Service is in our blood!"

The Pirbright Cleaning Co's van was a familiar sight in Dinham's streets, but somehow I had never made the connection. A fair bit can get past me.

"You're not here sniffing 'round my Poppy again, are you? She's upstairs doing the bogs, but I–"

"Good God no!" I butted in all too loudly. "I mean to say, erm, sorry, we're here on business, Mr. P."

"You? Have business? *Here?*"

"We were told to come and measure up the ballroom for the wedding, matey?" schmoozed Lotto.

Pat Pirbright gawped at my friend as if trying to complete the most cryptic crossword imaginable, clearly uncertain what to make of the Lotto style – the whisp of bleached hair arising from shaven bonce, Sid Vicious apparel loosely housing a long thin body with barely a curve to be seen.

"Oh yes, the rocker band," the vinegar-faced cleaner held open the door at last, and his face drooped like a slice of rancid spam being tipped into a bin. "Well, you should have said."

"When?" Lotto asked.

"When you just did."

"...Sorry!" we replied, and stepped inside the cold and echoing hall. With a cluck of disapproval, wee Pat bustled off on some sanitary duty, and we goggled. My infant memories of all the cartoon trappings of the stately homes of England, rusting armour and all, were so quickly proven to be unusually correct that I laughed out loud.

"Swish. Hole!" Lotto gasped, gazing up at all the faded tapestries and sad stag's, boar's and bear's heads which loomed over the cavernous great hall. Ancient weaponry splayed metres up to the rafters, and alongside them, row upon row of golf clubs of some vintage. Oil paintings of long-dead nobs who were no oil paintings stretched out below them, and the musty air was heavy with dusty privilege.

"Watch where you're stepping, I just cleaned this hall – in fact, shoes off!" Pat fussed from afar, and so we padded in socks to the enormous ballroom, twinkling in the dusty light of twin chandeliers.

The colourful Lady of the Manor from the news report was straddling a mat before a monstrous fireplace, apparently engaged in some kind of Yoga for the SAGA crowd.

"Oops! Hello hello, if it isn't our local din-makers! You must be Banjo Wako?"

I assured her that was the case, and introduced a still open-mouthed Lotto, who fought against whatever latent aristocratic awe was setting in with a stammered "Hullo there, your... your... missus."

"What a treat to have some talent in the house after so long," Lady Bobbie huffed, rolling onto her feet and giving us both effortlessly invasive and hot squeezes. "I think it's just wonderful that Terry has booked you to make his nuptials swing. It's so wonderful, isn't it? Since dear old Izzy McIzmo got spliced to Georgie Blandwood up at Blemsworth, it's become all the rage." A year or two earlier the glam rock god and High Priest of Suede, Sir Izzy McIzmo, had finally come out after a lifetime of marrying and divorcing blonde models, and settled down with his husband in this other big castle up in mid-Salop, up near the Wrekin – the freak finally tamed, apparently.

"'All the rage' is one way of putting it," Lotto said, "but perhaps people are just discovering the freedom to love whoever they love?"

"Darling, you put it so much better than I ever could," her Ladyship smiled, "The other groom is Geordie, which is an absolute scream. We're going to let this old pile sing for a bit, one last time, while we can. You know, I crept into the Angler's one night and saw you play, I'm sure. You were wearing sunglasses then..." She peered at me. "I never realised. Those eyes!"

I blushed, as if she would have noticed.

"Anyway, you're all a scream, do set up your whatevers and test the acoustics however you like!"

Lotto began to take a more technical look at the room's capabilities, which Lady Bobbie apparently took as a cue to lead me arm in arm around the Castle, brandishing a gigantic smoothie which she seemed to have plucked out of the air.

"Welcome to Yaxley Castle, Banjo," she began, "Gaff of my family of awful fumblers for most of the last millennium, one way or another."

We strode through mahogany hallways and past vast rooms tinkling with crystal, and every corner seemed to offer irresistible potential acoustic experiments. We entered the library, and while my hostess had a fiddle with her phone, I picked up a book at random:

*"Of the two antithetic terms in the Greek philosophy one only was real and self-subsisting; that is to say, Ideal Thought as opposed to that which it has to penetrate and mould. The other, corresponding to our Nature, was in itself phenomenal, unreal, without any permanent footing, having no predicates*

*that held true for two moments together; in short, redeemed from negation only by including indwelling realities appearing through..."*

I slammed the book shut. If that was the kind of stuff these people enjoyed in their toilet time, perhaps I was in the wrong place.

"We had always really been rather lucky, or certainly, father and Bill had the best advisers," Lady Bobbie went on, "So we haven't had to worry too much about the place falling down, eating catfood out of tupperware in the lodge and so forth. Yaxley still stands. There have been Mannerings and Phippses here for nearly a millennium, you know? Earls of any number did their bits at Crécy and Agincourt, and returned home to Yaxley to lick their wounds and toast their victories, and, I don't know, eat swans or something."

I came face to chestplate with a huge chonk of a suit of armour which had clearly seen better days a few centuries earlier.

"Yow. Now that's a big boy," I said, and lifted the visor just for a routine check that Scooby Doo wasn't hiding inside.

"That would be one of the Mannering-Phippses who fought at Agincourt, I imagine. There's history stinking up the place in every corner, darling. But sadly, since my dear silly brother Billy bought it, Yaxley Inc has now become a slice of prime real estate just waiting for a takeover. Do you play golf?"

"Um, a little crazy golf at Rhyl when I was a kid, but no."

"Ha!"

"I can tell you, if I played golf my handicap would be that I didn't really want to."

"I don't mind the game, really, I've had plenty of fun in the rough in my time, but I'd rather my home wasn't converted into a nineteenth hole by a gangster homunculus. You heard about the Van Hurl business? We're shrieking after lawyers trying to find some loophole."

Out of a creaking door stage right creaked a voice: "Roberta, what level of intimately private family detail are you planning to barf all over this fellow?"

"Now, Angela–"

"Who are all these people? So much traipsing, up and down."

"They are the band?"

"The band? Musicians? Do they need to be here before the wedding? It's bad enough that our home should become a wedding venue, without letting just anyone in for a free guided tour."

"Angela, don't be a snob."

"Why not? I miss proper good old-fashioned snobbery. The quality of snobbery around here is so inferior these days."

"I'm sorry?" I interjected. Yes, interjected, no less, I've checked.

"But – manners first, of course. So, hello, Banjo Wako from the band." Lady Angela turned on me without a smile and accepted my awkward head bow. "Your eyes!" she whispered.

"Yes, we've had that, my eyes, yes."

"Well. Well, may I ask why you are so fascinated with my family's history and legal predicaments?"

"Um, well, I don't recall actually asking..."

"Oh, come off it, Ange," Bobbie bawled, "Everybody knows everything that's going on, that bilious beach bozo makes sure of that! Besides – this chap here is the nephew of Faiza Malone, who we agreed was an absolute darling, so why shouldn't he learn more of the Castle he's playing in?"

"Oh yes, Faiza Malone's nephew, please do pass on our regards," Lady Angela actually smiled a little, and it was surprisingly sweet. "Tell her from me – it's purring like a panther again!" And the twin sisters clucked like tickled hens.

"That Afrikaan blob! He says he used to holiday here with his mother, but I know I don't remember hide nor hair of his arse nor wig."

"A distant South African branch of the family," Lady Angela asserted.

"As I understand it," Bobbie swooped in, "Daddy often called himself 'The Last of the Mannering-Phippses'..."

"But he did have these twin cousins..."

"We never met them, but they were always known to us as Uncle Clod and Uncle Useless – anyway, they were both so annoying..."

"Wasting the family fortune, chasing after chorus-girls and whatnot."

"So they were both packed off to South Africa a whole hundred years ago, as families did with their dirty little boys back in those days."

"A hundred years ago, in the twenties!!"

"How funny it still feels to say that – the *nineteen*-twenties, I beg its roaring pardon."

"The way the facts were outlined to me," intoned Lady Angela, "they were endlessly ill-behaved in London between the wars, and they were a great deal naughtier in South Africa. They were to work in oil..."

"And of course the bastards had zero principles, and so they hit black gold, got it all for themselves, and built up this huge fortune. Angela, I'm going to tell him about Lala Van Hurl."

Her desaturated twin clucked again. "Oh, if you must. Look, this here is the billiard room, but we do also like to keep up to date, as we have a space invader somewhere..."

"This girl Lala Van Hurl was swept into the orbit of Clod and Useless – call girl is my guess. Big. Blonde. Bouncy. The old boys were well past their retirement age by then, well into plastic pants territory..."

"One of them in a wheelchair, I believe."

"Anyway, after decades of devotion to harvesting their gold, these two twins suddenly turned on each other..."

"As twins so often do..."

"Now, come, Angela, you know I love you to smithereens, darling. But Clod and Useless were at war – at one Johannesburg charity do, they had to be ejected for brawling on the dance floor. It was all in the papers."

"Yes. Then came the death."

"Ooh, you do set the scene, love. Very conveniently, Uncle Useless had a cardiac – so the private doctors said – leaving Uncle Clod ready to scoop up the girl, and head off into the sunset, with Lala lovingly pushing him..."

"...Right into the path of a speeding tank."

"A complete accident, of course. Little Troy nothing but a particularly disgusting babe in arms."

"That poor woman, clearly she couldn't catch a break."

"Then a few more of her marriages took them from South Africa to New York, the pair of them inheriting left, right and centre, until she finally carked it about twenty years ago. We never saw sight of them in the family..."

"We had some vague idea there were branches of the family tree abroad whom we had never met, but now..."

"But now here we are," Lady Bobbie concluded, as we re-entered the ballroom. "Suddenly at the beck and call of a raging Wall Street racialist..." It seemed she was still on verbs, but her sister broke in.

"My daughter was telling me, some of the nasty groups he is associated with... those White Knights, they call themselves... our dear family name is going to be dragged into the mire, Mr. Wako!"

"I ask you," her sister added, "how can you be a white supremacist on a scrap of sun-burned land where white people have only lived for a few generations? It's like being a pheasant a mile underwater shouting at the fish for ruining everything."

"All that nastiness can NOT come from our branch of the family!"

"Of course this whole shack should really belong to us, and our daughters," Lady Bobbie swept on, "But the old Yaxley problem", the twins turned to me and chorused: "Nobs with no knobs."

"Women have never been allowed to inherit," Lady Angela spat. "Our Papa was an absolute darling, and as you probably know, he lived to be over one hundred..."

"A hundred and five, he was – the poor darling hit his first ever hole in one, and the shock did for him."

"... But in all that time, Papa never got round to changing the set-up one bit. And then our brother dear Bill, the sixteenth Earl, you know, he was already stricken in years when he came into the title, and he always said he was going to fix that nonsense, legally, but..."

"...But if he ever tried to keep more than one thing in his mind at once, Billy would forget how to drink his tea. It was often said that Bill had been dropped on his head as a baby..."

"Because he certainly was! Reggie told me, he saw Mummy drop him. She and Daddy had been to see one of those awful American Football games on one of our family New York jaunts, and she got over-excited trying to demonstrate a match-winning goal kick."

"Poor chap seemed dazed for the next seventy seven years... Do you know, it was on that very banquette there that Ozzy Osbourne asked me to marry him?" Bobbie sighed, gesturing to a dusty old couch. "It simply wasn't on, though. He was married. And also, of course, brummie. But I can't help feeling that he was never quite the same after I turned him down, he went rather off the rails, really."

Ordinarily rock anecdotes are like Banjo-nip to me, but I found myself distracted by a vast painting. Entering from this direction, the whole space seemed dominated by a terribly fishy canvas, gilt-edged in a blocky frame and unfortunately eye-catching. The portrait was of a young-ish dude, perhaps a bit younger than me, with goggly eyes and little or no chin, resembling some ancestor of Plug from the Bash St. Kids, in his Sunday best. He peered through a monocle and the googly face behind it had this oddly drooling prospect, like a pedigree poodle fixated on a big fat sausage.

"Well, he looks, er, hungry, doesn't he?" I ventured.

"Oh, that's Daddy when he was young. Mummy found the portrait and gave it to him for his seventieth birthday, almost certainly because she knew he absolutely *hated* it. Apparently it had been used for some kind of soup commercial, but we've never found a copy, have we Ange?"

"No, never found a copy."

"Ooh, it's you, Banjo – the wicked Faerie King himself," came a voice not from either aged twin, but an unexpected corner, and a sight which made me jump like a frog on a hotplate, which I assure you is no place for frogs. Had I known that Poppy – her tresses now hacked into an arrangement of blonde, purple and lime green – had begun earning a living by assisting her Dad in the broom-pushing business, I might have been more prepared. The last time we had shared oxygen, she had been streaking off into the night declaring me too gullible to suffer. I was still feeling the glow of relief.

There next to Poppy was Lotto, but looking unlike the Lotto I had left a few moments before. The poor sap was whiter than ever, with eyes like shining moons, and obviously a mouth as dry as dust. I'd seen that look before, and tutted. Lotto was in bloody love. Again.

"Hello, hello, *hello* and hello!" I helloed Poppy, and saluted so embarrassingly I had to try and pass it off as a mosquito attack.

"Long time no hugs, Banjy-Wanjy. I never would have thought of you as a nob-sucker, you know, sweet one. Right now I'm having to work for my Dad to pay my way to India, but I've had my eyes opened to the privilege of these places, so if it wasn't for India you would never see me dead and decomposed in a – what did my wizard friend Darrell call it? 'A graveyard of inherited greed and colonial exploitation and–'"

"I'm sorry, but shouldn't you be hoovering the dining room or something, young lady?" Lady Angela sniffed.

"You see?" Poppy said with a terrifying sudden grin, eyeballing her temporary employers. "I'm on my break, sweetheart. We are allowed those these days, we peasants." Her eyes flicked over to my technical director, who was standing there with a drooping plug extension and nipples like daggers. "Who's your friend?" Poppy purred.

I had forgotten that during my time of trying to untangle myself from the Pirbright's tentacles, my right-hand person had been completing a Masters in Music Technology at Dundee Uni, so the two were strangers.

"Oh, I'm sorry – Poppy Pirbright, this is the Dinham Drones' lead axe-person and technical whizz, Lotto Jenkins. We're just here to recce for the Scholfield wedding."

"Whoosh, sweet boy, this castle is a bit of a step up for the Drones, isn't it?"

"I'm sure they will all be marvellous!" Lady Bobbie broke in, "We can't wait!"

"I think I can," her sister added. "I do hope you will be able to resist too much of this 'doof-doof' noise they all like these days?"

"Lotto, are we planning to 'doof-doof'?"

I had never actually seen someone 'gibber' before, but assumed it involved monkey noises. Lotto somehow managed to stutter a few such syllables – "Doof-doof? No doof-doof" – and I knew it was time for us two salt-of-the-earthers to retreat to normality.

With promises to provide a show worthy of Yaxley Castle's awesome privilege, we bowed out, and left by what I guess was the tradespersons' entrance.


A good friend is not just one who knows what makes you tick, but will actually put up with all the bloody ticking. Lotto seemed testy, and broke an awkward silence.

"Banjo," they began as we wended our way down the gravel paths onto the Dinham road, "You knew this Poppy?"

"Well, yes."

"Knew her *well?*" A certain steel entered Lotto's tone.

"Well we knocked about a bit, a while ago, you know what I mean?"

"But nothing serious – of course, nothing serious, how could it have been? She must have been experimenting in some way..."

"Lotto, you know I'm not a man who discusses these things, you were away in Dundee, you know, and I felt the episode best left silent. You know, I go for the Girl Next Door type."

"Yes, because you're a lazy get!"

"Har-de-har. Look, honestly, as your oldest pal, I don't know how to put this, but my dear person, Poppy is an absolute–"

"Goddess of the Forest!" Lotto spasmed.

"Oh, Lotto Lotto Lotto. Please come back down to Earth."

"I first saw her at Ancient Rain..." my moonstruck side-axe went on, referring to the vegan bistro over on Corve Crescent, all incense and pea milkshakes, a definite 'Poppy peril' avoidance zone for me. "But every time she's been there, right in front of me, looking like Titania lost in the West Midlands, I can just never quite work up the, I don't know, the gumption, to say a single word to her. She moves through the world like a synchronised swimmer through a sea of champagne!"

"Please don't hit me, Lotto, but as your best pal of almost a lifetime's standing, you do have a tendency to flip for the very worst women."

"Wash your mouth out with Vim, Banjo. The only thing plaguing me is why such a Goddess would want to meddle with you. She must have been experimenting. Yes, yes, I'm sure, she may have been drawn to your celebrity sheen, Banjo, but thankfully she must have seen the error of her ways and now is just waiting for the right person to..."

"Lotto, as your friend–"

"As my friend, you must do something for me, Banjo. If you and her are still friendly enough... could you put a word in for me?"

Now, friendship is all, has always been my motto, but this seemed to be taking every last drop of piss. I drew breath between my teeth with intent. "Look, soul sibling, if you wish to make the same mistakes I have made, you're a grown dude – just go and ask her for a drink."

"How could I dare? She has this look–"

"I know that look, like a tripping seal."

"What did you say? She's the most beautiful woman who ever existed! Have you never seen her sideways?"

"Maybe, but look, Lotto, sometimes, beautiful people are like a beautiful countryside view – looks well enough from afar, but right up close it's just a load of shit, barbed wire and horrible scratching things."

"You can't sway me, you know? Seriously, Banjo, this is it. I have never felt love like this before. Everything that's ever been sung about love, from shang-a-lang to WAP, I feel it deep in my groin. I just, you know, any time she's there in front of me, my mouth turns into some sort of shoe-lining. Be a pal, give her a shout and put a word in for me."

"She showed me her Tinder profile once, and she did say she was sapiosexual."

"Well, this sap is bursting with sap for her, my old friend."

"But Lotto, you've said all this to me before, about Big Bella from The Hot Crotches, and Mrs Harris from the WI?"

"Oh, Banjo, the fancies of youth! Poppy belongs to another realm entirely. Just say something nice about me, then lay it on thick about my breaking heart."

"You cannot imagine the awkwardness of approaching her, my dear sap. Can't you just suck it up? Let it pass? Some other tender goddess will be just around the corner, you know how you–"

"Are you trying to insinuate, my dear Banjo, you, my best pal since we were kneehigh to a Marshall amp, that I am what some would call 'a ho'?"

"Lotto! The very idea. It's just that you do have a tendency to romanticise–"

"And I thought you were a friend."

"But I am, I am!"

"So you will go and do this very simple thing for me? As a friend?"

"Oh, right..." I said, with a feeling of impending bum ache. "... Ho."

## Chapter Six

Texting a woman you spent countless yonks trying to flee from is a tricky business. It's made worse when, within a few hours of bumping into that woman, she has sent you a monochrome selfie with the words 'BANJO I SEE BENEATH YOUR SKIN' emblazoned across it in neon letters. I buckled down to the phone and tried to do my best.

'Hi Poppy! What a surprise! My friend Lotto says hello! Would love a bit of a chat?'

Came the reply, 'Bet you would...' and then a pulsating ellipsis which somehow mesmerised me, until a bag of pork scratchings to the head reminded me of where I was, and I ordered a stiff cocktail to gird my quivering loins. (A Bakewell Pornstar, thank you for asking – amaretto and cherry coke, tastes like liquid Mr Kipling. You're welcome.).

My thumbs slowly hammered away an approach to this icky task. 'This friend of mine, they have this breaking heart xox—' I had typed, when a dramatic slosh of scrumpy from the neighbouring table, where Pete was belting out 'Don't Stop Believing' with surely excess abandon for half-past six in the evening, caused me not only to cack-handedly type those last three letters, but also – horror of horrors – thumb 'Send' too early.

Again, the pulsating dot-dot-dot...

'Fine. Meet me by bog bridge 7pm xx'

My thumbs trembled to explain further, but it was no good. A smiling thumbs-up GIF was sent, and I took a gulp. I suppose at least I hadn't mis-typed an aubergine emoji.

The genius scheme agreed on with my childhood buddy was simple – I would take the lady in question on a bit of a short walk, talking up Lotto's considerable attractions as best I could embroider them, and having done my best to liquify her with longing, Lotto would text me to give me an excuse to vamoose, and then move in on a thoroughly warmed up audience – they having loitered behind the bushes at bog bridge from 6.55pm. It was a classic set-up, nothing could possibly go wrong. I texted Lotto with the info, downed my drink, and aimed to make like a sycamore.

Just passing through the snug was JJ, AKA Mrs's J's daughter Jemima, recently returned to the comforts of home like so many of us well-ripened millennials. Strikingly tall, like her mother, with thick black hair and thin black suit, and only the faintest whiff of ex-Goth, JJ was somehow part of that fine establishment, but also a bit of a novelty, to me at least. She, like Poppy, had attended a girl's school somewhere out east, and all we tended to know about JJ is that she had spent her twenties picking up BSc's and MSc's and doctorates of all sorts from cities around the world, pulling pints to pay her fees, until only recently returning to head up the family's 'research development' – brewing beer and 'experimental' Buck-Up lines. This massive maze of a pub gave her space somewhere out beyond the old brewery to tinker with flavours and brewing processes, but only rarely was she seen down here amid either hoi or pilloi.

"A very good evening to you, Banjo. Clement for March, isn't it?"

"And a wop-bam-aloo-bop to you too, young JJ, and yes, what brings you down among the mainly metaphorical spit and sawdust this unusually balmy night?"

She barely glanced up from her clipboard as she answered, "I have been summoned for a family confabulation, up in grandfather's study. I can get somewhat wrapped up in my researches, back in the lab."

"Ah, some new flavour of Buck-Up in the wings, is it? Avocado and damson? Venison and Vimto?"

"I'm sure I could crack Vimto, if that's a customer request," she replied, with undue kind sincerity. "But, no, nothing in that line, it's – I had better, actually..." She gestured up the winding stairs behind the bar. "Abscond. Another time, forgive me." And I waved her off up the stairs.

Having never had parents, the concept of *grand*-parents seemed even more weird to me. Despite positively having my own buttock crevice carved into the old place's stools for years, it was easy to forget about the Angler's old landlord, surely long gone now, but in bygone days perched somewhere up at the pinnacle of the sprawling alehouse, where there was a kind of crow's nest affair which must surely have boasted incredible views all over the town. I recall Mrs J mentioning that she was past forty when JJ came along – her eldest, Jasper, from a previous marriage, being some kind of Professor of Cleverness in Yale or Harvard or one of those places. Judging from the old photos tastefully framed and displayed behind the bar – long-forgotten fishing trips, festive parties, Home Guard platoons and the like – Mrs. J's old man must have been pretty well seasoned when he first took over the Angler's Rest.

Stepping out into the nippy spring evening, I dipped in my pocket for my Zippo and had a couple of entirely necessary quick ones on my trudge to Bog Bridge, a well-lit green spot near the by-pass, bordering onto the barb-wire-bound Yaxley bog, a field so continually drowned by the river Corve for so many eons, all us Dinham kids knew to leave it well alone, unless a real winter freeze made it worth a dare. This small grubby dog-walking spot and barely functioning play park still had the weathered steps of some ancient gazebo, where once no doubt lords of the manor plighted troths to damsels soon to be in distress, before the field became council property. Now its grubby green paint flecked off in the evening breeze, and blew away on a wafting wave of skunk.

I could see a disturbance in the bushes, and popped over to gee up my lovelorn pal. "Keep still, dude, what are you playing at? Just wait here, and I'll do my best to prepare the ground."

A grunt or sneeze from the leaves was all the answer I received, before an unexpected wolf whistle told me that we were not alone. I slowly spun around, and sprawled there waiting for me was the eye-tantalising sight of Poppy, thumbing through a book with Homer curled up awkwardly on her lap. The grouchy hound was grizzling in his sleep as if the two had been sitting there for hours. "Poppy, Poppy, Poppy!" I ventured, attempting a neat vault over the back of the bench to sit beside her, and promptly tearing off a damp corner of rotten wood, landing arse-down on the grass with a ker-thunk.

"How still and peaceful everything is," Poppy grinned, eyes glistening up at the stars visible through the orangey suburban glow. "Oh, look! You can see the Great Gnome in full tonight, it's so clear. And look at that little star all on its own over there. I wonder if it's lonely. Is it part of the Dolphin's Smile?"

Poppy had deep interests in what she termed 'astronomology', belief in the power of the stars to decide our fates – but only using her own names and charts. "Orion's Belt looks nothing like a belt, after all," she insisted, "So I see connections in the stars which make much more sense, as this universe expands – the Great Gnome, the Paintpot, the Winky, and more!" She assured me that, being born in June, my star sign was Bungle, which apparently means I am very trustworthy, depending on what I am asked to do, and that I have good teeth.

"Ah yes, the bloody old Gnome up there," I replied, "I think I can almost see it except for this street light. Bloody, bloody old gnome. Um, talking of lonely stars–"

"I know you don't have faith in anything. You'll find this impossible to believe, Banjo, but you're really very cynical, you know. Duh! You wanted to see me, to draw me in to your web of naughtiness again?"

Her aspect was, as ever, that of a woman in expectation of something extremely juicy. I could think of few more cringeworthy duties than the probing of a well-estranged ex as to their attitude to gender-blind romance. The tightrope walk of seeming the most basic perv was going to be a saggy and death-defying one.

"Er, yes, we were talking about lonely stars. Well yes, now, erm, see, there's this aching heart here in Dinham, young Poppy, and–"

"Don't call me young. Typical patriarchal flup-flups. I'm only five years younger than you."

"No, well, yes, sorry, what I meant to come out with is, there's this heart, you see, and it's sort of aching."

"New lyrics?"

"I mean, you see, I have this... friend... and they have made it clear that they have fallen head under tummy in love with you."

"Well, why don't they tell me so themselves?"

"Gumption. Would do, but can't. Bursting with sap every time they look at you, but just can't seem to whack up the, you know, the zhuzh, to tell you."

"Oh, Banjo, you are funny. I think that's what first drew me to you. Life is so very sad, isn't it?"

"Well, it certainly is for this aching heart I was going on about. You must have met Lotto, my right-hand person. They – *they!* – they're an absolute genius, good old Lotto is, they're um, tall-ish, and thin, and they know a surprising amount about newts, and, um, what I'm having a good stab at saying is..."

"Please tell me you're trying to set up a threesome with this girl."

Her eyes shot nuclear twinkles my way, and each felt like a direct hit on my spine – I should have known if there was a wrong end of the stick to be waved about here, Poppy would grab it with both hands.

"God, NO! With my oldest pal? Yeuch! And by the way, Poppy – Pronoun Police."

"Oops, pardon me, not girl. Oh, interesting. What's that over in the bushes?"

They seemed to be rustling more than ever. What was Lotto up to? "Lotto!" I cried, urging them on to pop over and make an entrance. "Lotto – ah, they're great!"

Poppy changed the topic – I think. "I must tell you," she said, "I'm becoming very seriously interested in polyamory."

"Are you? Well, I'll have to tell them that, then. A better girl, er, person, is in the frame. They will remain heartbroken, but..."

"No, it means... Well, actually, it's this old book I'm reading which is making me wonder – have you read it?"

I glanced at the faded eggshell blue cover. "*Spindrift*, by Florence Craye. Not found its way onto my bedside table as yet, that one, sorry."

"I found it in the Castle library when I was polishing. Looks totally unread. It's written by some old aristo, which usually would be a reason to burn it if you ask me, I wouldn't read anything by a nob, but something struck me in it. She seems to have sown the seeds of polyamory long before it was accepted as the natural form of love. It's all about this woman – this Lady, I suppose – cursed with incredible beauty, who decides to use it to torture and manipulate every pathetic man hanging around her, and some women too. It's eons ahead of its time."

"Bound to be on BBC1 some Sunday evening soon, then. About this aching heart..."

"Banjo," she replied, her eyes wider than a baby deer taking Optrex, "You know I cannot resist you. I am in the market for a primary partner. I'll give you another chance."

My kidneys rattled. I tried to speak, but just the sound of some kind of pained rhino emerged from my throat. The thing is, when a woman stares right into your eyes and says, "You're mine", it just seems somehow to go against every blob of blood in my system to turn around and say "You reckon?" Nonetheless, I made another brave stab at straightening things out: "Oh no, really, sorry but, um, you've totally–"

"I wonder if your Aunt Akifa is right after all, there might be something in you worth watering."

"Oh no, really, I'm fine for watering, honest, totally grown, I promise you. LOTTO!"

"Stop saying that."

"Okay. Lotto!"

"You know I still find you irresistible."

"I'm old enough to be your relative!"

"What you need is just a little coaching in how to achieve personal fulfilment."

"Sorry, but I've had just about enough of personal fulfilment, personally."

She arose and glanced at her phone. Homer twitched, and growled. "I really have to go, I'm meeting up with an old girlfriend from school. But To Be Continued, my Banjo Bear. When would you like to woo me?"

"Woo?"

"How about Friday night? 9pm, your place?"

"Woo?"

"Perfect. Come on, Homer, my sweet, it's time to pay a visit to Dark Sister and go hunting for white stags!"

She suddenly leapt onto my lap and folded me in such a wet embrace, it felt like the watering had already begun. It did, I admit, awake something in me. Something which had slept wrong, got a cricked neck and just wanted to go back to sleep.

"Ta-ta for now, my big Papa Banjo Bear", she waved, yanking the dog on its way before it could decide whether what it had just witnessed required him to tear off my face. I just sat there, like a popped waterbed, and watched her walk away with nothing more than an "Um, yes. Be good!"

I sidled over to the bushes. "Lotto, you child of a cowing girl-dog, where the frig are you?! I just did everything I could, but–" With a delighted squeal, the biggest cat you've ever seen outside of a zoo pounced on me, knocking me once again onto the filthy grass. I recognised the gigantic Ginger Tom as Biffy the 5th, resident mouser at the Angler, out on one of his expeditions. He looked like a cat had somehow devoured another cat entirely in one huge gulp, and then that cat had been swallowed by Biffy, and the obese old bird murderer lay on me with what I knew was affection, but it still felt like a winning wrestling move.

Once Biffy had deigned to get off me, we strolled together back to his home, me explaining my woes as we went, but it was no good – if the big old moggy understood me, he clearly never gave a shit. I returned to the Angler's snug, and slapped a plastic note on the bar. "Double scotch please, Sonya."

On the side of the bar sat Mrs J and JJ, business meeting complete, sharing a pot of tea.

"I found Biffy the 5th out by the bog, but he's home and safe now," I reassured them. "Also, overshare: I think I might have inadvertently just got myself a girlfriend." I probably grimaced.

Both women paused, before replying in harmony, "Congratulations?"

"I mean, I never set out to – oh, balls, Lotto hasn't come in tonight, have they? They'll kill me!"

"Allow me to ascertain your drift before it drifts away, Banjo," replied Mrs J, "But if I may offer a hypothesis, it sounds suspiciously as if, once again, some impressionable young groupie has vaulted into your lap, and naturally being the parfait knight that you are..."

"...You are planning to gaslight this unnamed paramour into believing that you *are* interested in them, hoping in eventuality to simply ghost them away without any even preliminary attempts to give them a genuine expression of your feelings?" JJ concluded with what almost amounted to a smirk.

"Indeed, all that", her mother added.

I couldn't help bridling at this. The unvarnished truth is one thing, but it could at least be sanded down a bit first. "Well look, I don't know, I'm a bit dizzy, but you know..." I heaved a vain sigh. "I mean, it can't be all that bad," I shrugged, valiantly, "She is undeniably a fizzy pip of the top bracket after all. Let's look for the positive. She... has curiosity. She is colourful. Bubbly..."

"One should always take great care around 'bubbly' people," JJ interjected. "In my personal experience, if you happen to shake them up and then take their top off, you may suddenly discover that you have a great deal of cleaning up to do. Things can get rather sticky."

I groaned. "I'm not sure that I'm looking for true love after all."

"Not when 'pretty convincing' love will do?" Mrs J set down her cup. "I can only conclude, dear Banjo, that you really must be terribly easily pleased."

It was time to down my drink. "If you say I'm easily pleased, Mrs J, then that's good enough for me," I retorted, and I meant it to smart. "Have clement evenings, won't you?"

I could see that I was going to get little support or commiseration from the staff, so with no regulars in sight, and no bar snacks whizzing through the air, I bowed out of the Angler's for the evening. I gazed up at that strange long cylindrical room at the top of the building, and remember seeing the corner of one curtain swish. It gave me a pang for family, and so I called Auntie Faiza, hoping for some kind of constructive advice on my romantic awkwardness, perhaps even kindly sympathy. Which means I really must have been off my bloody nut.

"YOU STUPID WET BOY!" my late mother's kid sister boomed, so loudly that the presence of any actual phone seemed somehow irrelevant. "If you want the girl, take the girl, be kind to the girl. If you don't, say so! What's the matter with ya, ya bloomin' 'ayporth?"

"It's a question I've asked myself, auntie!" I admitted, "I just don't seem able to say no, like it's some kind of – I don't know – badge of honour that I can't tarnish, somehow, letting someone down, especially a wom–"

"Oh yes, especially a woman?" came a cackling laugh from somewhere in the background of the Dudley homestead. "What a genteel knight you are, Uncle Banjo – you can't let this girl down, so you're prepared to gaslight her into oblivion!"

"Viv?" I cried, "You haven't been listening to all this?"

"Course she has, you arse, you're on speaker phone! Viv is trying out her new fusion dish for GCSE Food Prep – *Umfitit en croute*!"

I could positively smell the rich spices she would be using, and my mouth began to water. "And Uncle Tim? How's your indigestion?"

His Irish croak came over loud and clear: "A bit better, thanks, Banjo, anything Vivvy cooks agrees with me. But as for this other mess of yours, you can keep me out of it, ya dirty bollocks!"

82

"Sometimes you force me into the ridiculous position of almost agreeing with your Auntie Akifa, boy – you need to get over this habit of yours of turning into wet toilet paper every time a woman bats her bosoms at you, find the right girl, boy, person, whatever you like, and get settled down. You're always welcome here, but you need your own nest."

"He's not eating a bite of anything I've cooked if he's going to go round ghosting innocent girls!" Viv boomed, sounding more like her mother than ever, "Sort it out!"

"Yes, yes, I will, of course I will," I stammered back – regular face-fulls of Viv's cooking being one of life's main boosters. I wish I could have been there to tuck in to the sizzling hot meal there and then, but I let them get on with it, rang off, and returned home for a pot noodle, a little late night jamming and a spot of dreamless kip, preparatory to the next day's funky nuptials.

## Chapter Seven

I've never been one to blow my own trumpet, though I will loudly play my own kazoo until the day I die. With that in mind, trust me when I say that the wedding gig at Yaxley, once I kicked off the evening with the traditional scream – "BIG SHOUT OUT TO THE NOISE ABATEMENT SOCIETY!" – turned out to be one of the Dinham Drones' absolute zinging best. This, despite the usually averagely reliable Lotto being ridiculously late to join the lineup, and in one of their dazes, if not tizzies. Had Poppy gatecrashed the reception or something and put them off their game? Thankfully Mx Jenkins was at least toffed up to the nines like the rest of us Drones as befitted the occasion – I had even dusted down an old gleaming pair of white spats I had found in one of Dinham's many charity shops, and from spats to shades, I must say I was looking very much the part, and keen to get on with the show.

"Lotto, you bugger! Where did you get to last night?" I demanded.

"What? I never got your text until this morning! I've been working on a new project, and slept twelve hours, but listen, Banjo–"

"Never mind listen," Neville put in, "They'm literally waiting for us to start playing, old shag! I wanna get pissed as a cart horse!"

Glad as I was to avoid the inevitable psychodrama of my right-hand person discovering that I was now somehow re-dating the goddess they so loudly worshipped, we blasted into our smooth romantic tracklist with a kind of pent-up boom, the braying grooms taking their first dance to

'The Man I Love', and feeling our way around the crowd's moods, Love ever the theme, covering The Temptations alongside Slade, Pet Shop Boys alongside Shirley Bassey, every tune a floor-filler. Astonishing flavours of celebrity were seen swinging each other around the palatial hall: panel game comedians, right-wing Labour MPs, reality successes, Spice Girls, TV chefs, Joan Collins, the lot – plus of course, my Auntie Faiza, grabbing all the content she could for *Women's Stuff*. We players writhed among them, drums coming from one corner, guitar swelling from another, dancing as we sang and played.

It wasn't until a break was announced for the grooms to set off on their Alicante honeymoon around 11 that we sweatily got a chance to talk off-mic and compare notes.

"Cutting it fine this evening, weren't you, young Lotto?" I raised a sweaty eyebrow.

"Not at all – I've been here since the ceremony."

"Really? But I didn't see you–"

"Banjo, my dear dude, there's a gigantic something I think I should probably tell you."

"Now, Lotto, please, let me start by apologising from the very bottom of my very bottom, I–"

"You're apologising? Does that mean that I don't have to?"

"Why are you apologising? I was going to say, about Poppy Pirbright–"

"Oh really, Banjo, I thought you claimed never to bandy women's names around?"

"Sometimes the odd bandy happens when I'm not paying attention, I'm sorry, but you have to understand..."

"Banjo, Banjo, old friend of mine from the sea... why are we digging up these old childhood whims? My romantic life is a long and winding road, and you're referring to a crush I experienced when I was nothing more than a toddler?"

"It was only the day before last!"

"The scales have fallen from my eyes."

"Eurgh, I should hope so, sounds revolting. But Lotto, you don't really mean to say that after all I've been through, you're no longer interested in... PP, the self-reclaimed MPDG?"

Lotto squinted a moment as they unravelled the acronym. "I'm a grown person, Banjo, I'm a lover and sometimes my love squirts out in strange directions. What I felt for Poppy–"

"Bandier!"

"What I felt for the MPDG was nothing more than the virginal twang of a misbegotten young innocent."

"You lived in a bedsit with a PE teacher called Dawn for two years."

"Banjo, please don't dead-girlfriend me."

"She's not dead, she lives in Swindon."

"I mean, don't bring her up, it's disrespectful."

"I thought that was one of the things friends were for."

"What I'm saying is, I can no longer speak of what mistaken tugs my heart had ever experienced, until..." Lotto checked their watch. "4.55pm this afternoon. When – *she* – arrived."

"Oh, God. Lotto. Don't you *dare* tell me that you've just fallen arse-under-ankles in love yet *again?*"

"For the last time. I promise. I know. Just to speak her name alongside mine, it's so obvious – Lotto, and Talisha!"

"Talisha Scholfield-as-was? My dear Lotto, you don't mean to say you have pounced on the vulnerable ex-missus of today's celebrity groom, in the midst of her ex-husband's wedding?" No matter where on the gender spectrum Lotto felt most comfortable, when new female pheromones filled the air, they were always prone to turning into Olivia Newton-John in Act I of *Grease*.

"Oh, she's ecstatic about the whole thing, Banjo – she gave him away, literally! I promise you this time I have found my all, my–"

"Lotto *sweetieeee!*" rang out a loud and volubly lubricated fruity falsetto. "Where have you got to, my string-plucking rock star...?"

There was a thump, and the smash of an upset tray of glasses.

"I think I may be needed. We're all done for tonight, yes?"

I nodded my assent.

"What was it you wanted to tell me, by the way? About last night?"

"Forget there ever was such a thing, old friend," I sighed, "go and do your knight in shining armour bit, I'll help yomp the gear home in a few mo's."

"Spoken like a true pal," Lotto beamed, and bawled: "Here I come, Taleeesha!"

I was thoroughly off the hook with my oldest friend, then – but skewered, kicking and screaming on the dynamite Poppy Pirbright. I sloped off to the rear car park area to have a J and check on the van, and the sudden whoosh of what seemed to be an airborne beard trimmer very nearly took a chunk out of my carefully coiffured 'do.

"Sorry, Banjo!" Pete grinned, from the back of the van where he was manipulating a large and clunky remote control.

"Voom! Eh, 'at's alright, that, shag!" Neville was watching amazed at the flying skills of both Pete and his teenage son, Ziggy, who was fiddling at the controls of a whirring drone of some description, Pete keeping one eye on his laptop screen. He grinned back at me as I looked over his shoulder at the fuzzy blobs which seemed to fascinate him so much.

"Taking our band's name a bit literally, much?"

"Yeah, well, maybe, Banjo, but we built this here drone from scratch, saved up for every screw, it's got everything! Heat vision, night vision cam, and here's the thing – I'm looking into what strength of speaker we can incorporate into the little bugger, and Lotto reckons we can offer this new kind of ever-moving surround sound to every gig!"

"Is that the gimmick Lotto was losing sleep over? Wouldn't the thing, surely, end up smacking into dancers and slicing throats open or something?"

"Not with this lad on the controls it won't!" Neville laughed, "He's like Top Gun with a remote, s'awesome."

"Depends on the venue really," Pete added. "We don't always play ballrooms like this one, do we?"

We took it in turns to have a lark about with the contraption, until my own captaincy of the drone led to a narrow miss of the left nostril of a prominent panel game show presenter.

I was just about to signal the need for home and bed, when the crunching of gravel silenced us. Most cars had long departed, with only a few diehard party-goers still happily sloshing the stuff down back in the castle. Then a crackling heralded the sudden arrival of what looked like a Presidential Cadillac, with small white-crossed flags fluttering on each side, gleaming in the light from the ballroom, seemed to crunch to a halt with a sinister warning note, in D minor. I lowered my admittedly unnecessary sunglasses as the passenger door opened, and none other than PCSO Sam Blount hopped out in his usual grimy fluorescent vest to open the back door, all-but saluting as a suntanned brick of a creature arose, with his own pointless shades doing nothing to conceal that face again – the obvious mush of Troy Van Hurl.

He noisily unloaded his colossal frame from the back seat and oozed that lofty bulk up to its full nine feet nothing. He wore the same badly cut suit with white tie, but his orange face was at least partially covered by a pair of mirrored sunglasses which no doubt cost the same as a few months' family meals from a food bank.

Dark though it was, he took in the huge crumbling edifice of Yaxley Castle, and the scenes of diminishing dissipation echoing from its ancient halls, he took in the buzzing drone, the rusty old van, and finally settled his gaze on me. He lowered his own unnecessary shades and fixed me with a perversely piercing stare. We've all heard of people with eyes like pissholes in the snow, but for those eyes, the pisser would surely have to have eaten a whole bunch of rotten asparagus, and fallen victim to some kind of hideous kidney infection.

"So, this is my Castle. I am the King, these guys are my knights... So what are you, boy? The jester?"

He called me boy. Nobody does that, or at least nobody except one of the two women who brought me up. I was so taken aback, I had no immediate answer.

"Pissholes in the snow!" was the best I could muster, and the snickering Circular Sam stopped grinning at his new master's jest, and looked terrified.

The drone sank to the earth, and all was suddenly silent – even the late night party playlist had run out.

"What is this, drugs? You selling drugs here? My boy Inspector Blount here said there's some weird shit going down in Dinham."

It was Neville, never one to be impressed by bullies, who stepped in.

"Oi, there's a kiddie right here, mate – and nobody's doing any drugs. Well, you know, not the really bad ones."

"I – hate – druggies." The new Earl of Yaxley seethed, and picked up the drone. "If I see any of you little bitches dealing around my town, there'll be no need to find a prison cell for the scraps of offal which remain after I have torn each of you limb from limb and sinew from sinew like a pizza with strings of god-damn mozzarella." The plastic drone began to buckle in his bullish grip.

"Well, like my colleague says," I piped up, "Nobody's doing drugs. We're the band."

He lobbed the drone back at me. "Well you're sure as shit banned now. The party's over, boys, I'm-a givin' you the count of ten..." growled Van Hurl with the clearly carefully styled grunt of a Texas cop and KKK stalwart kicking Smokey and/or the Bandit out of the state. Had he been chewing tobacco, I am sure there would be a splash of it on my spats right now. "... Get off of my land."

## Chapter Eight

If you want to make God laugh, tell him your plans. In a really silly voice. Was it then that the real bomb dropped? It wasn't even technically spring, but suddenly everything changed – for the very worst. You can't help but twig and dig exactly what I'm getting at – no doubt by now endless literary awards have been dished out to numerous Virus novels, tales of death, hardship, isolation and valiant masked queuing outside the nearest open corner shop.

Well, I won't type a syllable to underplay the absolute disaster of the twenty-first century's first great pandemic. It was hard for everyone – but for a musician? Entirely reliant on the hot and sweaty vibe generated by the tools of my trade, in numerous cadaverous clubs, pubs and dungeons worldwide? Wile E Coyote strolling halfway over a crevasse had more chance of reaching the other side than I seemed to, survival-wise. Every festival pinged off the calendar, every tasty pocket-money-providing open mike slot poofed into thin air, and Spotify informed me that I was due enough royalties to buy a pot noodle – but only an own-brand one. And you can't just run away from your troubles. In my experience, they have to be constantly bribed to stay away. And, as they say, when one door closes, there's loads of closed doors everywhere. Takes ages trying to get the right one open. If you can, get a doorstop.

There ain't no party like a non-existent party. Friends were furloughed, but who could furlough me? You could have knocked me down with a silver hammer when I tentatively checked my bank balance, and saw a very generous recent input from YAXLEY ALES LTD. I had little time to sweat over it before a tinkling on the phone came courtesy of Mrs. J.

"It only seems a merited stipend, Banjo."

"But really, Mrs. J, it's too much."

"You should know by now that you are considered in no small way to occupy an almost familial role in our little empire. Those friends thou hast, and their adoption tried, grapple them unto thy soul with hoops of steel!"

"I like that, one of your own?"

"The brummie Bard, dear. You'll forgive me."

"But there must be something I can do to, ugh, well, earn it in some way?" I wondered. I'm not afraid of hard work. Just a little unsettled by it.

"We must all simply endeavour to more fully ascertain just how dreadful this virus' spread will be. Daylight is good at arriving at the right time."

"George Harrison."

"George, as you so rightly say, Harrison. Just take care of yourself, Banjo Wako. We do need you."


Still, it seemed a tad cheeky, living on a stipend. But if you find yourself left to your own devices, I say make sure that your devices are in full working order, and well oiled. Who knows, maybe some stretches of shit creek have some quite pretty scenery?

93

'Only boring people get bored' is a tiresome thing only ever said by very boring people, who do not realise how boring they are being. So I kept the ennui at bay, moving to the rhythm, I designed some absolutely triumphant face masks based on our album covers, and even sold a few online. I patiently shopped for Auntie Akifa and let Apple out to do his business. Of course, I vamped on some new chords, but it was tricky to find any lyrics to summon up the international mood. Had we been a goth band, no doubt it would have been a doddle. I just had to keep *doing* something. It's hard to watch the world go by when it just stands there. And glares at you.

Social distancing did, I admit, have some slight benefit when keeping the polyamorous advances of the pansexual Pirbright at whale's length. As I may be saying too often, I hope I'm not the sort of son of a sod who takes pleasure in toying with anyone's heartstrings, so in a way I was glad she had mentioned this scheme of spreading her devotion around a little. I asked no questions, and it goes against my – I want to say pride? – to go into detail in this exclusive tell-some memoir.

Cutting to the nub, that Friday night came and went, and once the shock of lockdown had settled down, the Banjo-Poppy misunderstanding morphed into yet another long-distance relationship – which these days is basically signing up to be someone's Tamagotchi until the batteries run out. I swore that when we could be face mask to face mask again, though, I would screw my courage to the sticky place, and reclaim my bachelorhood. Sometimes, a man's gotta get round to what a man's eventually gotta do.

"Banjo! That inky perisher of yours has been sniffing round here again, boy!" Auntie Akifa squawked as I entered with the shopping and gave it a squirt of disinfectant. "Why don't you bring to yourself a good God-fearing girl?"

"Cowardice turns me off, auntie."

"Don't get clever!"

"Then what else is life for?"

She shot me a double-barrelled look, which as ever froze me like a six-foot Vienetta. It would be too much to say that I dared to raise an eyebrow to her, but somehow the obvious fact that I was doing pretty much everything for them both allowed the matter to drop, the odd sneery grizzle from Apple aside.

That evening I inserted a pretty damn smart fluorescent paisley stripe in a new pair of forest green overalls which badly needed accessorising. I'd decided that if I was going to earn a wage from Yaxley Ales, then I was going to make myself useful in some tangible way, and the costume of a working man was a challenge to break the monotony. It couldn't be that bad, could it? The W word?

It was just as the light began fading and whatnot that a colossal banging on the door shook me out of a flat funk, and there she was, on the doorstep – certainly the physical form of – Poppy Pirbright. Green lipstick smeared over chin and cheeks, minuscule muppet fluff fur coat sticking out at all angles, just like her brown-and-pink-spotted hair, and eyes like still-spinning fruit machines.

She screamed, and ran at me. The shock of the moment makes it hard to recall, but I think she yelled something along the lines of "WHERE MY BEAR THERE MY BEAR! RRRUFF!" and launched herself onto my unprepared form like a xenomorph out of a party popper, encircling me and driving me down onto the carpet with a whoomph.

"Poppy! Lovely to see you, of course, but we've got this bubble, you see, because of the virus..." These were words which failed to connect anywhere as she continued to howl like a husky huskie for around a minute, before pulling a face and conking out sideways in a total blank.

I stared at my sort-of girlfriend's form, as utterly stunned as any dog-walker happening on a cadaver could be. Luckily her heavy snores quickly dispelled any fear that anyone would be stabbing at the number 9 that evening.

But stunned I still was, with justification. The virus' danger and the need to wash your hands to the tune of 'Happy Birthday' (or, my preference, 'Tutti Frutti') and whatnot was one of the few things which fully took root in Poppy's brain – which was a tangled-up graveyard of conspiracy theory twaddle, true, but having watched from a laptop as her cousin Ben went from strapping young bricklayer to box of dust in just a fortnight meant that nobody was taking the need for sensible social distancing more seriously than Poppy, or so she had told me from

96

wherever she was hunkering down. This vagueness had, of course, been a godsend, as her number one ghost Tamagotchi.

"WHAT THE SATAN IN SHREWSBURY ARE YOU DOING IN THERE, BANJO BOY?!" came sharply through the connecting wall, snapping me from my daze, but having zero effect on Poppy's apparent coma, and I could only stammer "Sorry, auntie, off to bed now, nigh-night!" and examine the snoring but beautiful corpse now laid across my rather tasteful Morroccan carpet. With less than minimal medical training, I tried my best to gently snap Poppy out of her sleep, but it eventually became clear that the only recourse open to any decent Not-That-Guy who wanted to escape with his good name intact was to gingerly carry the patient to my bed... and pyjama myself for a night on the settee.

My unexpected guest not having stirred through a quite loud, herbal solo evening of every unseen music documentary on the BBC iPlayer, I eventually dropped off well into the early hours, only after ensuring a large glass of grapefruit juice was by my bedside should Poppy awake in need. After deep and heavy dreams of being swamped in the furry black wings of giant butterflies, I awoke to a slam of my own door. By the time I could inspect all crib corners, not a sight of Poppy was to be seen. Just a scribbled note on the kitchen chalkboard – 'LOOK AFTER COW' – which set me to puzzling for most of the time between the first pint of coffee and the aural irritation of the radio news bulletin, a never-ending drama of blues which had to be filtered out somehow before they did their best to swamp any sweetness and light which could be dredged up. Skip to the music.

Another day of streaming media and strumming Minnie, limply lolling around the flat as the sun skanked down outside, simply did not appeal. And as I always say, if a thing is worth doing, it's worth doing eventually. Freshly scrubbed and splashed as I was, I slid into my working man's outfit, rolled a couple of tea-break Js, and decided to put my best foot forward. Admittedly, I did first have to decide which was of my feet was the best, which took an hour or so, but then it was brewery ho!

Pete was enjoying a vape break in the sunshine as I hopped over the wall into the brewery yard, resplendent in my forest green overalls with go-faster stripes, and caused him to break into what I hope was an appreciative bout of hysteria.

"Bloody Bowie Almighty, Banjo, what have you come as?"

"Worker Wako reporting for duty, Mr. Mulliner," I saluted, scooping up an idle broom and making a great show of scuffing it up and down the yard a bit.

"This is the first I've heard of this, mate. You, doing the W word? It's not often I'm struck speechless, which is what I am right now. But fill your bootees if you feel the need, man, I'm just off to the Sheet for a delivery." The Sheet, on the opposite edge of town, constituted Dinham's Industrial Estate, where a vast factory did most of the making and packing of both Yaxley Ales and Buck-Up in all flavours. Even working at half-speed, with furloughed staff swapping socially distanced shifts, the supply of beer and Buck-Up had to continue. So Dobbin and I briefly narrowed the distance between our elbows, and he zoomed off.

There was the odd crisp packet, corner of cardboard, and fag-end bringing down the tone of the yard, and so I diligently pushed them up and down a few times, throwing in the odd Fred Estaire sweep with the broom for good measure, until the honest sweat upon my brow suggested it was surely time for a well-deserved smoke break. I was taking the first puff when a voice rang out from the doorway of the tragically shuttered pub.

"Banjo, may I enquire what in the infinite spectrum of human existence you believe yourself to be doing?" JJ, arms folded, surveyed me as if I was an unexpected delivery of offal to a vegan picnic. Or perhaps she was getting as close as she gets to laughing hysterically, it's so hard to tell with that family. Inscrutable, is the word. Or it's certainly *a* word. "Please do come over here to within a two-metre distance, if you would, by sheer happenstance I do find myself in such a position as to need to grill your brains a little. May I?" Her eyes had honed in on my J, and taking the cue, I proffered the fragrant splee, but then our eyes met. "Ah yes, not actually the most advisable notion any more, is it, sharing? Simply irresponsible in the current climate. Distinctly regrettable."

You could have whopped me with a large-ish stick, I must say. Bad of me to judge people so quickly by their own outer casings, but Dr. JJ was not the kind of woman I had imagined was up for a puff. Clean and controlled, she always seemed, but it is quite often the quiet ones. "Would you care to take the tour, down into the bowels of the lab?"

"Bowels? Why not? Masks on?" I presumed, proffering my own. I think I was probably rocking my new The Artist Formerly Known As The Artist Formerly Known As Prince tribute 'Purple Rain' face covering that day.

"Masks on," she agreed, "plus hair-net, if you don't mind?" I carefully entrapped my 'do in the aforementioned net, and was led across a threshold I never had cause to cross before, into a new area of the Angler's – like unlocking a blank section of a map in life's long RPG. Silver canisters filled the shelves, and dazzling strip lights shone brightly down on the whitewashed rockery of the old pub's brewery. The white space ballooned out, like a vast badger's sett, carved into the rise of the hill towards Yaxley. A huge wall was covered with barrels and stills of all colours, all bubbling away to make their own unique happy juices.

"As you will no doubt have ascertained, this is where we house a typical batch of each of the major brands of ale currently in circulation, along with sample batches of current lines of Buck-Up. Do you know the history of Buck-Up?"

"I seem to recall Puggy Berringer living on nothing else throughout his GCSEs and ending up frothing at both ends in the middle of the Maths exam?"

"Of course, we attended very different schools," JJ replied. "But the beverage is without debate not recommended as an exclusive diet."

I made another mask-muffled attempt. "Didn't Dobbin – sorry, Pete's great-great-grandfather invent the stuff to kill dinosaurs or something?"

"If you drop a 'great', you're part of the way towards the truth, yes. Around a hundred years ago, it was first synthesised under a similar but rather silly name by a colonial chemist, Pete's great grandfather Wilfred Mulliner, as a specific designed to stimulate the nervous systems of Indian elephants. That was until a bottle of the tonic, still in its experimental stage, fell into the hands of a cousin of his, and the extraordinarily energising properties on humans became apparent. It works by stimulating the red corpuscles, to put it in the vaguest layman's terms. By the 1960s, heavily diluted carbonated versions of the formula, now finally renamed Buck-Up, were first passed as suitable for consumption by the British Board of Food Standards, and fizzed onto the market – sorry, I used to help out with the open day tours at the factory, force of habit. Follow me, Banjo..."

And, unbelievably, having somehow strolled into the bowels of the Shropshire hills, she clattered in a passcode to open yet another doorway, moving from the sharp white brewery into a far more cosy, cave-like room, softly lit by desk lamps and clearly not for public view – JJ's inner sanctum.

"Welcome to the Top Secret lab," JJ said, flicking on a monstrous chilly air conditioning unit and peeling off her mask. "I think you'll be safe to remove the mask here, but it's entirely your decision. I know that the woman you're ghosting is Poppy, by the way."

I stiffened. Was this an ambush?

"Hey, now, JJ, I do have to wonder if the word 'ghosting' is–"

"Banjo, I am aware, more than most people, that Poppy can be an anthropological and biological challenge at times, unless you are in possession of a particularly strong mind."

I think she had just called me thick, but I remained muted. JJ busied herself crunching out plastic labels on one of those old-fashioned letter-punching machines, affixing them on different clear bottles from time to time.

"The two of us were best friends – perhaps only friends – at St. Monica's, until the regrettable incident of the psilocybin muffins and the school gymkhana. We found this luscious yellow fungi growing by the stables, and as a budding scientist, I was fascinated to discover they were *gymnopilus junonius,* one of the most potent hallucinogens you will find growing in the British Isles. If I am to bear full witness, I would have to admit that it was Poppy's idea to actually bake the muffins. So when she ended up taking the wrap for the whole, what could be termed, *contretemps...* and it was her idea to give one to the Mayoress, I would have definitely advised against such a course... an instant expulsion was carried out. I was fortunate enough to go on to achieve straight A's, and on to Oxford. So I must admit to a certain degree of guilt whenever we happen to come together, which is growingly seldom. Dear Poppy gets these sudden fixations – you're an off/on one, believe me, Banjo. I think the answer is for her to take some time out again, which I will happily pay for, as a director of this company. It seems the least I can do. Not least because events have now taken something of a turn for the *deja vu*."

"You've lost me now, JJ. Elucidate, please."

She moved over to a large steel canister, and peered into the contents. "My grandfather bought a majority share of Buck-Up from the Mulliner family in the late seventies. I believe they were glad of the cash injection, and my grandfather had invested his life-long earnings with the same scrupulous agility with which he liked to gamble. Bookies used to call him 'The Magic Butler', for his uncanny eye for form. It was the Buck-Up formula which fascinated him most, however. As a young man in service between the wars, he was known for his own ability to prepare what he referred to as a 'Gentleman's Pick-Me-Up' with his own secret recipe – raw egg, tabasco, brandy being the most obvious base mix, but with surprising ingredients. He always swore by this repast, and many others swore harder. And so over the years, analysis of the effects of this organic formula, and the original Buck-Up chemical structure, have been developing. Grandfather always maintained that the remedy has the most illuminating effect on those in need – care for a taste? Don't worry, everything here is thoroughly disinfected and virus-free."

JJ had pulled on plastic gloves and proffered a tiny plastic cup of reddish liquid my way. It seemed rude not to.

I don't know how often it might be that you have found yourself near a jet engine spewing plane fuel, and chosen to use the spot to light a fag. The effect of this big spoon of umami syrup must, I swear, have been a very similar experience. I felt incandescent armies of flaming-torch-carrying chemical compounds roaring through my every vein, and a scrunch of nerve endings shooting in and out of my extremities, before bouncing beautifully back into place. I began to perspire, and when I peered inside my mask, it was pitted with dirt I never knew I had, somehow squirted out of every pore. I have never had an instant sauna performed while standing fully clothed before. I somehow popped my eyeballs back into their red-hot sockets and gasped.

"Not so smooth." was all I could hoarsely drawl. But then – ping! – it's hard to describe just how my every sinew felt fresh and functioning on full throttle like never before. It was like a hangover cure for a hangover I never knew I had. "Yeee-*argh*!" I added, for clarification.

"We are still carrying out extremely tentative and entirely humane non-animal experiments on this solution, which goes under the internal name of YXJ404..."

"How about 'Buck Me Ragged'?"

"Extremely witty, thank you, we shall consider it."

"I feel I could run up the top of Everest and be back in Dudley for tea. That is an extraordinary buzz. It's, it's *enervating*, if that's the word I'm groping for."

"That's actually the antonym, I believe, Banjo."

"Oh, yes, you can taste the antonym," I replied, smacking my mouth. "But a bit hard to market, I suppose?"

"There are some considerable ethical questions to be asked about going public. This formula can, it seems, extend and improve the body and brain's performance and longevity, and when our tests prove the extent of its efficacy, it would be immoral not to find ways of sharing it with the world."

"I mean, I always knew Mrs. J was a cut-above, in the head jelly stakes, but I had no idea genius ran in the family like this. Can you settle an argument for me?"

"Why, yes, I–"

"Nothing specific, it would just be good to know someone with so much brain has my back for some future dispute."

"That's very gratifying, Banjo, thank you. But this is only the penultimate degree of confidence which I am placing in you. I will save taxing you with mycological and chemical details, but a year ago a little of the previous batch of YXJ404 was left out right here, in a petri dish. When I returned from my month's holiday in Madagascar, I was fascinated to discover a rich, probing growth of fungus emerging from the deposit. As in, an entirely new form of fungus, which, in time, I will have to present to the scientific community."

Perhaps my eyeballs were goggling slightly more than usual, because she seemed keen to suddenly skip to the end.

"To expedite the narrative, Banjo, I examined this fungus in detail, and found the deposits to be far from typical hallucinatory fungi, and wholly distinct from any cannabinoid, opiate or psychedelic substance I had ever come across in all my studies. And so I found it simply irresistible to explore the forms of synthesis I could extract from this unique substance... And I came up with these."

She proffered what looked like a small tin of travelling sweets, containing several amber boiled pellets, like psychedelic pear-drops, glistening in the strip light.

"Purely for personal use, you understand. It was Poppy who wanted to call them 'Ecstasy In The Evening', much against my advocacy, as their chemical make-up could not be more different from *methylenedioxymethamphetamine*."

"Ah yes, that's a 'me' thing."

"I would not advise you to try one."

I can't say I felt too chilled with the idea of having the name of my well-loved music night linked to any dodgy substances."Did nobody tell you, JJ? I'm really not a pill man. Strictly herbal, and musical."

"Now, of that I was indeed unaware, Banjo. We all have our favoured chemicals. Since we were children, Poppy and I have taken many trips together. The expansion of the human consciousness is something it is so exhilarating to capture in strict scientific form, my PhD in Neuroscience was – to, I admit, the disapproval of my family – entirely centred on the effects of hallucinogens on the brain. It seems to affect different people in different ways, based on the psychology of the individual. When we took this substance together, for me, I was suddenly intent, like never before, on fathoming every inch of my brain – I had the sensation of flying through my hypothalamus, examining every memory, every byte of knowledge in my compass; it was an invigoration I had never felt before. And then, when I finally regained consciousness, Poppy had disappeared. And so had the majority of this precious and potent unique batch of E.I.T.E.. And from what I have ascertained, some of the YXJ404 may have begun to find its way into somewhat concerning underground commercial arenas. Poppy has meant a great deal to me in my life, but her presumption that anything specifically nailed down is as good as hers has always been a concern of mine, and I am naturally keen to protect her from any form of danger. So, if I may ask, Banjo, have you seen Poppy lately?"

Certain hazy events began to take on a relative clarity. I explained about my bizarre evening, and how Poppy went out like a light, but was gone by the time I woke up that morning. "I swear on my very neck, JJ, I behaved like a person of absolute honour throughout."

"From what I have deduced, Banjo, I do not doubt it. But this is severely troubling, she has often been prone to going to ground like this, not answering her phone. Where might she have flown to this time?"

"Your guess is as good as mine, JJ – and my guess is *rubbish*. Sorry to ask, it's none of my business, but why did you put these bloody naughty sweeties in Poppy's way, or indeed take them yourself? Seems a bit suicidal."

"'The highest activity a human being can attain is learning for understanding, because to understand is to be free.'"

"Plus you like getting completely out of your bonce?"

"Spinoza."

"And Spinoza to you, too. I can't say I approve."

"Of course you can't, you have absolutely no authority to do so."

She was right, of course, I could just imagine the scene, two old friends from the posh school:

"Gosh, Poppy, what larks we can have now we're both out of school!"

"Yes indeed, JJ, you are my best friend!"

"And you too! Want to take a huge bag of drugs?"

"Well I have squeegied my fourth eye, so yes, let's get to work on the fifth!"

"What wizard fun! Bagsy you first!"

"Yum yum!"

"Does this bit qualify for passing the Bechdel test, d'you think?"

"I don't know, Banjo is making it up."

"Well now it certainly doesn't."

And whatnot.

JJ snapped me out of my daydream. "Poppy and I do tend to bring out the irresponsibility in each other, Banjo, it's true. And the discovery of the fungus proved too strong a temptation, to experience first-hand what further properties may be synthesised from YXJ404. Now I have defined the effects from one experiment to my satisfaction, I am adamant that once is entirely enough. I felt a total negation of control, of my free-will, I have never experienced anything like it. Having thankfully fully regained the correct arrangement of my cerebral furniture, I will write up my research notes, and return to the wrangle of how to place our formula on the pharmaceutical market, and perfecting the flavour of Creme Egg Buck-Up. But first I need to find the dangerous remainder of this one and only batch, and locate Poppy. I have pulled a few strings, and her usual place at Glossop's is in readiness for her."

"At whereses?"

"The Glossop Institute, a rehab centre near the Somerset coast. She needs time off from a number of addictions, including, if I may say so, yourself. Please endeavour to inform me the very moment you hear anything of her, Banjo..."

"Oh, and do rest assured," she continued, as she ushered me out, took my hair-net, and slipped it into her pocket. "You have absolutely no need to do Pete's yard work for him. You are furloughed, and once vaccines are rolled out and plans are put in place, you will be performing for us once again."

"Though maybe not at Din-Dins, if You-Know-Who gets his way?"

JJ's eyes almost rolled. "Banjo, don't even mention his name."

I didn't.

## Chapter Nine

Van Hurl, it should go without saying, was a name guaranteed to make all decent people sick. But even having kept well away from the usual twattering apps all my life, the new Lord of the Manor seemed to be getting harder and harder for me to successfully ignore. The saying goes that shit rises to the top. Social media has shown us that it's more of a lava lamp effect, with bubbles of shit at the top and the bottom, and everywhere in between. And sometimes it leaks out all over the place.

It seemed even an innocent rare foray into the town centre was not safe from the leathery hatemonger. Lockdown had just unlocked a whole new field of staggering spite and stupidity – the anti-mask brigade, and of course TWK, Van Hurl's sponsored assembly of 'good people, proud boys, patriots to a man' jumped on that gammon bandwagon like bigoted flies to white dog mess. It being illegal to travel further, Van Hurl – the anti-masker general – must have been frustrated to only have the Dinham chapter of his network to muster together for protest, but it was just my twisted fortune to choose that moment to mosey on past this moaning rag-tag bunch of puce skinheads and ashen boomers as they made their noise outside the pound shop.

BBC News was there to capture it all, of course. And I registered zero surprise on seeing the fluorescent bulk of Sam Blount, now ex-community police officer, having been dismissed due to sundry online offences – I heard he vowed to eat the Duchess of Sussex. Stripped of his badge of office as he was, Sam was still trying to look the part, up at the forefront in his official-looking scruffy hi-vis, gazing at his leader with girlish devotion. And was that the stunted form of Pat Pirbright I saw hiding behind a banner reading "FREDOM OF SPEACH!"? I wouldn't put it past him. 'NATIVE ENGLISH RIGTS'. another placard just about read. Then I stopped reading. Never let it be said that I am against free speech. But arguing in favour of racism, misogyny, trans hate etc as 'freedom of speech' is like demanding everybody should be free to twirl blindly down the street holding razors aloft.

The tanned tyrant began to exercise his all-too-apparent freedom: "Isn't it ironic? Don't ya think?" the blonde brute was grinning from what must have been his own portable podium. "The exact people you now see creeping around like sheep obeying what the Powers That Be decree are those who call themselves 'woke'! Now suddenly they're gonna tell us how to behave? Wear their stupid masks, keep six feet away? I want them more than six feet away from me, guys and ladies! The layabouts, the so-called rebels, the snowballers and the branflakes!" The few people trying to get on with their social-distanced shopping clearly had no idea quite where he was getting these non-buzzwords from, but his scrum of acolytes snorted like a herd of bulls, and he unfortunately pushed on. "Well! Whatever they think about the new normal, we proud members of the British Empire are rising up to stand up for what we believe in! Winston Churchill! Queen Victoria! Van Morrison! You know, one of the greatest, maybe the only real great, rock singer there ever was, I really mean that.

He never played that god-damned music festival, did he? Yeah, well soon, nobody will. For too long you good indigenous people of Din-Ham have had to put up with enough of these drug-peddling outsiders, these unpatriotic do-gooders who wanna tell us what to do, who would happily see the City of London crash into ruin rather than open up business, and get this beautiful country back on its fantastic feet again! God Save England!" More discordant moos. "And here we got a special message for you all, from my good friend, ex-BBC political editor – and yeah, I hate the Goddamn socialist BBC as much as you do – Mr Piers Clarkson!"

Even some of the bipartisan crowd clapped, at the sight of the famous TV face now taking the mic. Another professional hate-click merchant, with millions of followers, columns in two Murdoch papers, and a wife in the cabinet. It would be unfair to say that I wouldn't piss on him if he was on fire, I absolutely would – just not on the bits that were burning.

"Well what a beautiful town this is, Dinham, it's great to be here. And how do you think I got here? I DROVE! MY BEAUTIFUL 4x4 LUXURY ROAD ROVER SUV SPLASH!" Van Hurl's blotchy claque hooted at this show of pointless defiance, and I thankfully managed to steer myself around the corner, down towards home... when that voice drawled out of the shadows.

"Yo! Not your kinda entertainment? It's getting kinda popular."

I should of course have kept walking, yet I span on my heel and found myself in the shadow of the Chief White Knight once again.

"If you're so popular, why do I want to punch you in the face?" I wish I had said. Other subsequent dazzlers which later occurred to me included "I don't beg to differ, I just differ" and "If there is a heaven I hope your dear departed loved ones are looking down at you, and finding it impossible to resist an understandable urge to flob." Instead, "Six feet away, please", was all I came out with.

"You're the Woke-oh guy, right? I heard about you from my cleaning girl – that's a freaky piece of ass if ever I grabbed one. You were the shady dealers lurking around my castle."

"I have never dealt anything but... Top Trumps... and one-liners!"

"I don't care what you call this shit, Woke-oh, we got our eyes on you."

I suddenly felt like calling a policeman, and reflected that I may as well call for Deep Heat to rub on a sunburned knob. He approached, I took two steps back. Then Van Hurl said something which took me entirely by surprise.

"We sure could do with a cool dude like you to add to our ranks, ya know?"

"You – what? Me? And THAT?"

"Oh yeah, I guess you think we're all racists, right, that's what you got drummed into you? Well, it's official, boy – Britain ain't a racist country, and we are the real Britain." All this in a pained mix of Wall Street and Afrikaans which delivered the operative word as "Bridden". Again, he moved towards me, and I reversed to maintain maximum social distance. "With more like you on board, and in the crowd, well, it looks good ya know?" And he cackled snidely. "Maybe we can even talk about that Din–Din rock festival of yours. Make it a White Knight special? I'll scratch your back, you scratch mine, and we'll see who draws most blood."

"So you're an equal opportunity group of white supremacists?"

Now, this man may have been full of shit, but there was a great deal of him to fill up with shit to beyond bursting point, and I could as good as see his Orc muscles bulging under his suit. And yet I began to feel new spirit stirring somewhere in my marrow. In Dinham town centre, no less, I never foresaw a time when this kind of naked hatred was given a platform. This maniac was clearly mad, dangerous, and bad to know.

"I'd like to talk to you about everything and nothing, Lord, but just the latter is quicker." I was pleased with that one. "Besides, I think your Tory guest star is running out of gas, Van Hurl," I continued, referring to the petrolhead's diminishing shouting, "better get back up there. Find yourself another Uncle Tom. NAMASTE!" I said, meaning the exact opposite, and took the opportunity to trouser off speedily when his back was turned.

"Hey, DON'T HAVE A COW, MAN!" he bellowed to my retreating form, and then I was gratefully otherwhere.


Lockdown remained in every way locked down – an eternity of boxsets, shopping and aimless jamming. Trapped in this gig-less world, away from my dearest pals, let out of my cage only to queue up for provisions and the occasional burst of freedom out in the fields, my life's calling – the

114

sprinkling around of sweetness and light – was beginning to feel like I was standing on the hose. The real world kept crashing in so tactlessly, the radio news, the headlines – cops kneeling on necks, ordinary folk blown away by the force, all this wrought on those who just happen to be Black. And then the virus turns out to be twice as vicious for us as well? We have an actually racist pandemic? What on this side of the galaxy was going on? And as for your thoughts and prayers – if you're offering prayers, your thoughts can't be worth all that much.

The latte of human kindness suddenly seemed to smack of sour froth. I began to wonder whether there was only so much 'sweetness and light' could achieve, especially without the music blaring out in the streets, in the clubs, throughout the halls. 'First they silenced the poets!' Who was it who said that? It can't have been just me. Believe me, I do try to visualise a just society, but it's like trying to get turned on by a dead mouse.

One curiosity which did brighten these lockdown days was a sort of local boost for the DDs – even though of course gigs remained an impossibility – in the form of Auntie Faiza Malone's exclusive *Midlands This Evening* feature on a sudden twist in the legend of The Honourable. She having been granted an exclusive socially distanced interview with the great Izzy McIzmo up at Blemsworth Castle, I received a typically bellowing call from the quite intrepid reporter, asking me to provide background muso info. Despite the temptation of a spot of local exposure, I had to doff my beanie to Dobbin, the true Drone for the intricacies of rock and roll archaeology.

So there he was on my TV screen, my mate Pete Mulliner, denied his usual crook of the bar at the Angler's, but still telling his stories to half of the West Midlands, in front of his life-size cut-out of Frank Zappa. "The Honourable had this uncanny ability to remain in the background, but as confidante to a whole generation of rock and roll's greatest, he was a fixer who, in his own way, steered the whole course of this massive chunk of British culture, back in the sixties, and the seventies, right up until his disappearance. It's like every real rock spod in the world has been looking for him ever since, because, well, where could you look? So this new lead is pretty amazing, yeah." The caption below read: 'PETE MULLINER Rock expert and drummer, The Ding Dang Dongs'. My eyebrows shot up.

This reported rock revelation had actually come about because of the effects of months of lockdown, and the slow drying out of Sir Izzy's many-decades-sodden system, now that he had found love at last. An archivist had been up at the Castle going through heaped bin bags of McIzmo paperwork going back to the start of his career in the sixties, and discovered a thirty-something-year-old scribbled air charter for the private jet he had as a timeshare.

Lolling out in the spring sunshine amid the beauty of Blemsworth, the rock demigod confessed to my auntie, "I had absolutely forgotten it f–bleep–in' existed, Faiza, swear! And Elton must have been no wiser, because he never mentioned it to me neither, and it was half his jet! But we'd both of us, we'd do anything for The Honourable, y'know, he'd gotten us out of so many fixes on tours all round the bloody world, so when he asked to borrow the plane, y'know, I must have just given him the wink, and away he f–bleep–in' went, y'know... And I thought no more about it."

"Sir Izzy, rock journalists and conspiracy theorists have spent decades trying to work out where this shadowy backstage figure had disappeared to since he was last seen in the eighties. You're saying that you gave The Honourable Reginald Mannering-Phipps permission to charter a private flight, and he never came back?"

"That's right, he never came back. If it was any other f–bleep–er in the biz, I'd have presumed they'd nicked it, y'know, but with the Hon, you couldn't have thought that, he was a man of his word, bless his posh socks. As the moniker suggests, y'know? I wish I could remember everything about why he wanted to f-bleep-in' fly off like that. Where was it? Africa or somewhere. Asia. One of them."

"It's well known that Mr Mannering-Phipps had been a core part of the crew for Live Aid in 1985, and had spent some time in the Sudan in the earliest days of Comic Relief, helping to set up new aid routes."

"Yeah, y'know, I'm not sure either of those shows would have got going without Reggie busy in the back room fixing things up, going over there to make sure, y'know, the money was gonna go to the right f-bleep-in' places and that. But it's all such a blur," Sir Izzy laughed. "A total mental f-bleep-in' mess, the whole eighties, and half the seventies, and as for the nineties – I mean, did they really happen, when you stop and really bloody think about it? Apparently I duetted with Gary bastard Barlow – twice! Can you f-bleep-in' believe that?"

"Oh, you certainly did, my darling," piped up a reedy voice from under a sunhat to the superstar's left, where I don't think anybody had noticed his husband Georgie Blandwood, the 11th Earl of Threepings, was plonked. "Such a lovely ditty, that first one, how did it go? *Ditty ditty doo-doo... something along those lines.*"

"Lord Threepings, do you have any memories of the Honourable Reggie Mannering-Phipps, being the heir to the Earldom of Yaxley, a fellow Shropshire nob... noble personage?"

"Young Reggie Mannering-Phipps? Ahhh... no, not many, he was a little younger than I, my dear. Perhaps he was pals with my eldest, Lord Bozzam. His father was very bad at golf, I seem to recall them saying."

Cut to: footage of Yaxley Castle, with Auntie Faiza's purring outro: "Though Sir Izzy McIzmo's revelation seems to shed some light on the legendary disappearance of the true heir to the Yaxley fortune, lost somewhere between Birmingham Airport and Juba International over thirty years ago, no corroborating documentation has yet been traced, leaving this rock and roll mystery, an eternal riddle. Faiza Malone, Blemsworth Castle, Shropshire, for *Midlands This Evening.*"

In all truth, I must on some slightly misty level have registered the sheer wackiness of this new connection between the towns of my birth and my life, but other questions were bubbling up which I felt had to be dealt with first. I messaged our group thread:

Me: 'WHO THE GLENN MEDEIROS ARE THE DING DANG DONGS THEN?'

Neville: 'SOUNDS LIKE A RIGHT BUNCH OF TODS TO ME SHAG'

Pete: 'I SAID IT LOUD AND CLEAR HONEST! THAT PRODUCER MUST BE TONE DEAF'

Me: 'WHAT GETS ME IS A LEGEND LIKE MCIZMO NOW THINKS THAT'S WHAT WE'RE CALLED.'

Pete: "THE TALENTED CHICKEN IS THE GREATEST ALBUM OF JUNE 1975'

Me: 'WELL EXACTLY!'

Lotto: 'ACTUALLY EVERYONE, BAND MEETING?'

Neville: 'WHAT YOU MEAN BAND MEETING? I BEEN STUCK HERE HOME-SCHOOLING THE KIDS ALL DAY MATE!'

Pete: 'POOR BAIRNS'

Neville: 'WATCH IT DING DONG'

Lotto: 'I'VE GOT A REALLY REALLY HEAVY PITCH TO MAKE. RATHER DO IT IN PERSON. BOG PARK AT 7?'

Me: 'CAN DO. SHALL I BRING MINNIE?'

Lotto: 'WHY NOT?'

Neville: 'OK ANYTHING TO GET OUT OF HERE: MOTHER'S HOME NOW'

Pete: 'AS LONG AS YOU'RE NOT PLANNING TO PILE ON ME FOR THE DING DANG DONG THING I'LL BE THERE'

Me: 'ANON THEN!'

As I set off, I was jangled to receive a missed phone call message from none other than the Pirbright. Bizarrely, almost as if my phone was afraid to offer it up, it had been sent days before, and when I opened the file, its volume was almost Faiza-levels of deafening, amidst the noise of drilling and banging.

"Hello Banjo, my lovely treacle bear, I hear you've been looking for me, that's so sugary sweet of you! I do miss you terribly, you know. I'm sorry for shouting, but my Dad has me working at the Castle again, and the Beast is making what he calls 'perfections' to the Great Hall – the place is swarming with hi-vis-types! I just wanted to call to let you know that it's okay, I wazzed out for a bit, but I think I might accept JJ's offer of a holiday at Glossop's anyway, they do *amazing* cous-cous and I need to realign my chakras and vital essences. Yeah, my Dad can keep Homer in check, or the other way round. But as JJ seemed to be in a flap about it, I also called to let you know – frick, it's so bloody loud here! – I know pills and suchlike aren't your bag, my sweet elfin boy, and I didn't trust myself after that first trip, so I slipped the Ecstasy In The Evening into your robo-cow case thingy. Did you get that? I PUT THE DRUGS IN YOUR ROBOT COW CASE! OKAY? JJ'S SPECIAL SWEETIES ARE IN YOUR IRON-COW THING! Goddess Gaia, it's so noisy! I've got to go, my love from beyond the clouds, but when those clouds roll by... ah, grrr! Love you longest time, kisses, kisses, kisses everywhere, mmmmwah!"

Yes, a direct transcript.

Things were beginning to look a bit sick. The sooner I had those mad pear drops out of my cow and back in JJ's lab the better. But I was almost at the park, it would have to wait.

Somehow I was the last to show up at our rendezvous, with trusty Minnie in tow, excited as she was to jam with other people again, and the bombshell dropped by Lotto on my arrival was quite a toxic one. I hadn't seen my old friend look so rattled since that fateful day at their Mum's wake, when they had first announced that ultimately they wanted to be Freddie Mercury, but at the very least a change of pronouns and decision to transition was underway. Which I think we all took on board with all love, besides the odd confused throwback. They're always 'she' to Auntie Akifa. Anyway, Pete and Neville were as agog as I, and Lotto's eyes boggled in watery sockets as they pulled the release hatch.

"It may surprise you to hear... what you weren't expecting me to say." Lots of shrugging all round. "I think I know where we can get a gig... and we can pretty much name our own fees."

"To what tune, Lotto my old lad?" Neville asked. "I'm not cheap, I's'll tell you that for... a great big wodge of cash."

Lotto paused. "It's a Level 42-grade budget, apparently, if not Texas. I was thinking, if it all worked out as I envisioned, I wouldn't settle for less than twenty grand. Each."

Neville announced in essence that he would do some pretty unsavoury things to his late grandma if Lotto wasn't pulling our parts.

"The reason it's so high is because not only is the potential gig illegal at the moment, it's being thrown by someone with a money-to-sense ratio which beggars the universe. Now look, I'm not going mad. Troy. Van. Yes. Bastard. Hurl... Is planning a huge anti-masker party thing up at the Castle."

Oaths were seethed. Jaws wobbled. I turned on my heel – or at least, I turned around – and prepared to lug a disappointed Minnie back up to Wickham Mansions.

Pete laughed fit to burst: "You have got to be on something, Lotto, I preferred you when you were just whacked out on love."

Lotto called to my retreating form: "Please hear me out, Banjo! Old pal from the sea! We can work it out!"

I turned again. "Lotto Charles Jenkins, we have been jamming together since practically on the nip, and never did I envision you would have gone off your poor nut like you seem to have done now. The Dinham Drones? Playing an illegal rave for a bunch of anti-masker not-so-neo-Nazis? None of us would ever live it down!"

"But this is what I was thinking, man – The Dinham Drones definitely wouldn't have anything to do with it... but these people want The Ding Dang Dongs."

Somebody surely interjected an "Eh?" and Lotto whooshed on.

"It's all come via Talisha's ex-PA – she's now a party arranger, and in short she seems to specialise in do's for the more fascistic kind of event. That's why Talisha let her go, she couldn't afford a bigot on her books, but the two of them still happen to occasionally chat, and she mentioned her scouring the shire for musical cabaret performers..."

"With death wishes and zero morals?" I snarked.

"Exactly!" Lotto beamed. "I might as well kick the arse out of the whole thing at once by also admitting that the party is tomorrow night."

Three grown men exploded in torrents of derisive farm animal noises, while Lotto begged for calm.

"It had to be short notice – they'd originally booked those lute-plucking trust-fund folksters..."

"Oh Christ, not the Babcock Bros?" Pete groaned.

"...But one of them just got flamed off Twitter for some kind of 'anti-woke' joke, and their management pulled them out."

"I'd pull them out, given a chance!" Neville added, and we mulled over this for a few milliseconds.

"Anyway, here's the kicker – Van Hurl's been whining all over his social media about his inability to get Fox News up at the Castle, and he apparently watched that local report on The Honourable, and thought a local band would be the best solution, money no object."

"Maybe he took a liking to you, Dobbin," Neville jeered.

"I see no reason why he should do that!" Pete protested. White, bald, and undeniably potato-like as our drummer obviously is, it was obvious why Van Hurl would approve. His heart of jewel-encrusted gold, however, underlined ABC's old adage about book cover judgement. "I'm sorry, Lotto, if people found out I'd been part of some hate-spewing gammon gangbang, I'd have to move to, I dunno, Cumbria or somewhere."

"Sorry to say this, boys, but you're still working, Pete, and Banjo, I know the Yaxley lot have furloughed you comfortably enough."

"My thoughts and prayers go out to you, flap about a bit, fall on the ground and evaporate like the useless platitudes they are," I said. "Besides, I'm not that comfortable, without gigs I'm sinking."

"Well exactly! Nobody will know it's us, and just think of all that lovely moolah!" I eyed my old friend as askance as I was able, and they twigged the sting. "Banjo, just because I'm transitioning and in a relationship with a cis woman, it doesn't mean that I'm actively in favour of starving in the gutter. I have given my Talisha certain assurances, that I can pull my weight, financially, and a one-off payment like this will save my bacon, eggs and fried bread."

*"Girls don't like boys, girls like cars and money..."* Neville sang.

"No, Neville," Lotto replied, "That's mechanics you're thinking of there. Come on, you and all the little Nevilles must need a cash injection?"

"I'd rather a vaccine one first, but yes, of course I bloody do. But, my dear old shag... Christ, think of all the bastards who'd be there! If he's got all that bloody money, why dunnee just book Van Morrison and Eric Clapton?"

"Or at least Right Said Fred?" Dobbin added.

"Besides," I offered up another nub, this one a proper gloopy bogey of discontent. "There happens to be this massive horrible virus stalking the

124

populace like a coughing werewolf, Lotto. I'm not being forced into a sea of sweating skinheads, it's a suicide mission!" Some ideas are too preposterous to be pooh-poohed. You have to shit-shit them instead, and in the bud.

"We can make it safe!" Lotto persisted, "I've been thinking of all sorts of ways, we can be pioneers of socially distant performing! Remember I was working on something for your drone, Pete?" Lotto revealed what looked like a tiny bluetooth speaker, and began forking out tons of technobabble beyond my recording.

Eventually, Pete caught Lotto's loony bug. Frowningly, he ventured, "Sooo I just play my drums outside, and–"

"And the drone carries that rhythm all around the party space, without you having to set foot in the room! I was thinking, Banjo could be up by the one front window, all open of course, and Neville up the other, and, well, I'll just have to keep myself as distant as I can, I suppose. And I think it's a fancy dress do, so we can make sure we wear masks! I was thinking of Zorro. Then I realised his mask is the wrong side of his face, but I'll make a special beardy face mask."

"We can't sing with masks!" I shook my head.

"But we can try – whatever happened to looking at the bright side, old friend? The thing is, I'm a 'Glass Half-Full' person, and you lot are more 'Glass Overflowing With Toxic Waste Oh God It's Spurting Like A Volcano And Won't Stop And Some Of It Has Definitely Gone In My Mouth' kind of people. We can do this. Come on, one night as the Ding Dang Dongs, and we have a good year's salary in the bank."

I hung my head. "We're only in it for the money."

"Zappa!" Neville put in.

"Well, of course it's Zappa," I shot back. "And I say the best things in life are free, Lotto replies that I can keep that for the birds and bees. I've just never been motivated by dirty cash in all my life."

"Very, very dirty it is, too," Pete said.

"I know, I know," Lotto mopped their brow. "But the way I see it, the biggest bastards are winning, right, left and centre, in Number 10, in and out of Europe, and the biggest bastards are becoming richer, and bigger all the time. At least this way we're snatching a bit back for ourselves."

"Pick-pocketing the ogre, as it might be?" Neville mused.

Lotto laid a finger on their nose, and pointed directly at Neville. "We can really show the lot of them! Everything we do will be to mock them, and we'll get the cash up front. Musical agitators, detoxifying the most acrid of privileged patriarchal prick jamborees!" I swear by this stage there were flecks of foam at the sides of Lotto's mouth. "Come on, this gig, this is protest for payment, it isn't working for that bucket of scum, it's sticking it to The Man! Don't we love sticking it to The Man?"

"The problem with sticking it to The Man, is that it nearly always falls right off," I replied. But annoyingly, an idea had struck me. "I mean, I think I know what I could wear... but this is insane, Lotto!"

"That doesn't sound like the Banjo I have always known and loved. Where's your spirit of adventure?"

"It's socially distancing! I'm sorry, but it's a capital N-O. Like a bridge over troubled water, I will keep right out of it."

"Banjo, I am asking you as your best friend. We all are. Pete?"

"So I'm just drumming by the van then?"

"Well, if the ace drone piloting skills of Ziggy are available, yes."

"Yeah, Ziggy can't get enough of it. Four fat monkeys for drumming outside the van seems hard to say no to. Nev?"

"I got my Spider-Man costume, shag. Should blend in well enough with that lot of old restraining-order divorcees."

"Just one gig, completely anonymous. Please, Banjo, be a pal?"

"In twenty four hours?!"

"We know a zillion songs. We can brush up on a few online. I'll never ask for another favour ever again."

The grimacing faces of three dear pals stared up at me – and there, I felt it again, this exasperating internal tug of being incapable of letting a friend in need down. No matter how appalling the demand.

"Ugh, Lotto... okay."

"You give us your word, as a Dinham Drone?"

"Nope, only as a stinking Ding-Dang-Dong, but... yes. Socially distant, two hours max, with masks."

"You won't regret this, Banjo, old boy."

"Lotto, You are, as ever, the wind beneath my wings – blowing me into the path of a speeding articulated lorry. I wouldn't go so far as to call you a 'so-and-so', but you're certainly a great big steaming 'so'."

And so we began to put our plan together. There were a fair few flaws and imponderables to be worked out, but then we'd stop at those bridges when we came to them. Maybe have a sandwich.

"Benjamin, pray you tell me, what sort of friends are these of yours, these flabby white boys coming here, lowering the tone?" Auntie Akifa's greeting when I checked in before bed seemed unusually cryptic, rather than the usual "I should be a great-auntie by now" or "Why don't you get into care work, or something people want, rather than all that NOISE?"

"I'm sorry, auntie, I haven't any idea what you mean."

"The blasted children at number 19, they're always teasing and cussing over poor little Apple when he sits out for his evening sun, and this time he goes off charging after that ginger blighter, yapping and yapping, so I had to go out and call the boy back. Could only be a few minutes later, I return to all that banging and crashing in your room, there's these two strangers standing, bare-faced, here in my dashed flat. The fat police boy I knew, he said he was an old friend of yours but I thought even you had better taste than that, Benjamin. This big boy said you invited them round. Where have you been, boy, with that God-baiting virus out killing folk left, right and in the middle?!"

I charged through to my private quarters, and was initially relieved to find that nothing much was awry, besides my bass guitar which had fallen onto a host of bongos, badly denting one of my favourites. Akifa and Apple followed me, and both gazed around disapprovingly.

"They were no friends of mine, auntie," I replied, steeling myself to dare to suggest that in some ways my maternal relative may have been to some degree just a little bit at fault. "You know, you really have to be more careful..." I began, but then came that stare – the one which made Paddington at his angriest seem frankly wet-arsed. "Well, I'm sorry, but... burglars, auntie! Burglars!"

"How am I supposed to know, with the kind of perishing friends you keep, my boy? I remember the days and nights when you could leave your door open, and..." I was tempted to say, "Do you mean back in Juba, when an armed militia could be ramming through that door?" but thankfully she just grumbled on. "...And nothing bad happened. It's Godlessness, I tell you, Godlessness!"

"Well at least it looks like nothing's..." My eye finally fell on what should have been a glaring gap on top of my shelves. The IronCow special Silver edition vinyl doll and pencil case prototype, was gone. "... Shit."

"Banjo! How dare you use this language of the ghetto to me?"

"Sorry, auntie. I mean, nothing. Nothing's... nothing's nothing."

Where the IronCow should have been was a smudged post-it note, which read 'WERE COMIN FOR YOU–' and then there were two three-letter words beginning with 'N'. Some might say it was a more homely version of the main 'N' word, but it was no less revolting.

Having apologised to her twice for her own mess, and knowing no such apology was headed from the other direction, I ushered the two of them off to bed, and sat down to think.

These were such times when that elusive G.A. would have come in handy, somebody to unpack this parcel of rancid doings with, in a calm and intelligent to-and-fro. I sat down on my phone, and emitted a severe oath.

*"Okay, I found this for Falkland bus times..."*

"Oh, shut up, Suri."

The situation had gone from a pig's breakfast to a dog's dinner. I needed it to become a cat's snack at most.

## Chapter Ten

"Now you be so feckin' careful with this, my lad, treat it like you would the lady love of your life if she was made of sugar glass," Uncle Tim warned me, as I took possession of a vast old-fashioned astronaut costume, dome and all. "This was the ACTUAL space suit worn by Mel Smith in 1985's *Morons From Outer Space*! Stupidly, the bastards cleaned the snot off the visor, but I put some back on. Verisimilitude, y'see."

"Thanks for this, Tim, I promise not a stitch shall be out of place – it's for a socially-distant gig, you see, and–"

He let out a short, sharp whistle, and made a 'zipped' gesture with three fingers. "Whisht – no questions asked for family, Banjo. I just wish I could invite you home for tea – she's got a pot of Kamounia on the go, with Shaaria for afters."

"Ooh, is that the one that's like a coconutty pasta bake?"

"Exactly. I'll post you a slice in a jiffy, maybe!" He gave me a wink, and drove off home.

I had promised not a stitch out of place, I know, but our experiment in virtual band performance required Lotto to tape a number of tiny computer things – Rhubarb Pi's, I think they were called – into the space suit's inner lining, giving me a built-in head-mic and ear-pod tuned in to the rest of the band. I had found a kind of extended air purifying mask, a little too on the Darth Vader side, but it allowed me room to sing.

All the rest of the gig preparations were of course down to my non-gendered bestie, earning their Craig-David-rivalling evening's fee by having to actually hang around the Castle for most of the day, as the nation's worst congregated to toast their ugly contrarianism, or libertarianism, or in short, fascism. We had agreed to cue up a pin-sharp recording of our previous gig at the Castle, to blare out if anything went wrong and we had to bail, but Lotto assured me the whole shabby shebang would be like taking candy off a particularly generous baby, on a diet.

I tried to call JJ to give her the bad news about her stupid space sweeties, but only reached her answer phone:

*"You have reached JJ's voicemail, I would be indebted if you could provide a brief summary of your motivation in attempting to communicate with me. Thank you."*

"Ah, JJ, it's Banjo Wako here. The musical fella, you know. Look, I'm guessing you must be somewhere headed south-west to take Poppy to your funny farm – sorry, drying-out spa place – but I thought you might need to hear the bad news pretty rapidly. That is – it's vanished. The cow, that is. I had to head out for – reasons – and when I got back, someone had barged into my flat, and it was gone. Mind. Absolutely. BLOWN as to how anyone could have known what was in it. But I have a good idea of who it might have been. So – and I know this sounds absolutely BATTY in the circs, but we've accepted a hush-hush gig, we're kind of agitating against Van Hurl's anti-masker lot, and I reckon one of them will have it on the scene. So I'll rouse up all my Sherlock skills to the hilt and try to track it down for you, for all of us, but otherwise... erm, enjoy your rehab! Sweetness and light!"

I cringed a little at the closer, but it was sent, and I returned to perusing our chosen setlist for that night's journey to the sewers. After an awkward online rehearsal, and many reflections that on the whole, given the choice between providing the cabaret for a far-right jamboree and being insensitively mounted by a love-crazed rhinoceros, I would happily apply the lube and welcome Mr Horny with a smile on my lips, the calendar and clock crept towards Gig Hour. I couldn't leave all those little Mulliners and Sanderses without chicken dinosaurs on their table, nor could I let down Lotto. I just had to take a deep breath and hoist Minnie on my shoulder for a yomp up to Yaxley, and face – well, create – the music.

"After all," I told myself, "What doesn't kill you, may maim you for life or cause deep psychological damage."

I jumped over a stile which I knew would lead me round the back way to the Castle, preferring to be as unobserved as possible – I just wanted to get in, find the IronCow, earn lots of grands, and get out again. As questionable luck would have it, there to greet me were the Ladies Bobbie and Angela. There was noticeably less bounce in the former than at our previous meeting, and both wore floral face masks.

"It's just too bad of you, you know, Banjo, really it is!" was Lady Bobbie's muffled opener. "We saw your strange friend, and I said, it surely couldn't be that lovely lot, the Dinham Drones, performing for this bunch of bastards, but here you are!"

"And as a space man!" Lady Angela added.

"I know, I know, my dear ladies, but please, you have to bear with us," I lowered my shades. "We're sort of here *undercover*, you see, it's hard to explain."

"He's made me move out to the lodge with Angela!" Lady Bobbie pouted, and what was visible of her sister's face turned from vinegar to battery acid.

"Very charming," Lady Angela groused, "It's me who's had to move all my pickling jars to the shed."

"Yes, thank you, Angela, 'Pax!' I'm glad to have a roof over my head. But, oh, Banjo, darling, do you swear that you are not on this son of a shitberg's side? You're, what's the word?"

"Protesting?" Lady Angela offered.

"Agitating?" Lady Bobbie suddenly grinned, "Against these awful yobs scuffing the polish on our ballroom floor?"

"He's been clearing out all the rooms in the Castle!" Lady Angela positively sobbed. "The legal papers are only just zinging across on the emails, and yet he acts like he owns everything already! He seems to be building his own personal newsroom or something. He must be stopped!"

"And you have a plan?"

They both looked up at me with such hope shining out from their little aristocratic faces, I had to play along.

"Something like that", I replied, giving them full force of the blue eyes. "I promise you both, the Dinham Drones hold no truck with any of the HATE peddled by Van Hurl and his flabby White Knights. Hate is the only thing we hate. Hate, and Michael Bublé. Sorry! That was just a little joke. But honestly, I can speak for the whole band when I say that we prefer sexy and racy to sexist and racist. If the choice is between being right-on, and right-off, I know which suits me best."

"Oh, goody!" they chorused, and Lady Bobbie hugged her sister. "It's just like *Wind In The Willows,* isn't it?"

Lady Angela considered. "It is, actually, isn't it? Should I go and get, um, a rake or something? There's old Plank's gun?"

"Woah, no, best not, not tonight," I calmed the forces. "First we're going to give it to them with music. I'd better get into position now."

"So brave!" Lady Bobbie fluttered her eyelashes at me, and I crept my way around to a small side entrance.

How sweet it would be to just glaze over the most unwelcome show in the history of shows, even after so many months of missing the blast of music and the warmth of the crowds. The whole noise jamboree was planned out impressively by tech-mages Lotto and Pete, and only Lotto, Neville and I had to actually enter the building. I don't think Uncle Tim would have been too happy had I cut off the fingers of the space suit gauntlets, so I wore long fingerless gloves, my shades, my music mask, and two stripes of fluorescent paint across the bridge of my nose. The other two were similarly masked up in full disguise and padded all over with mini Rhubarb Pi's, waterproofed against sweat. And there must have been gallons of the stuff – Neville was a Shrek, and Lotto some kind of papier-mâché Zorro mess. Might have been the Hamburglar.

A millisecond before the designated starting time, I had received a text from JJ: 'STRONGLY ADVISE AGAINST PERFORMING TONIGHT. LIKELIHOOD OF SERIOUS HARM PERTURBINGLY HIGH. WILL RETURN ASAP. JJ.'

But by then I was already sliding my phone back into the inner workings of the costume, and flicking Minnie into life. There's something about the phrase 'You had to be there!' which usually makes me glad that I wasn't, but this show had to kick off. The white puddings were getting testy. I stumbled towards my chosen performing spot, and stifled a boak at what I beheld.

So this, I thought with a shiver, was the new roaring twenties. Classic tunes aside, I'm not generally one for nostalgia, but a shaded glance through my astronaut helmet gave me a strange tug of revulsion on behalf of the folks who had maybe cut a rug or two in this ballroom a century ago, the dear old goggly dudes and fizzy coked-up flappers who had rehearsed the latest whizzo steps over cocktails, back in the proper twenties. I mean, some of them probably turned out to be Nazis anyway, I know, but this is a century later, and where are we? Nazis all over again.

As I glared from the ornate ceiling down to the vast walls – conspicuously more bare of paintings and cutlasses than when last we were playing the Castle – the inheritors of the dance were hooting and brawling over the heavy tables of free booze and virus-riddled buffet.

What a stinking shower of misbegotten beasts this was for us to play for –
no, to, I prefer 'play to'.

There was that Ludlow-Starkey scum receptacle and his high-up White
Knight circle-jerk brigade, Non-PC Sam Blount was clearly on his third or
fourth layer of flop-sweat as he stood in the shadow of this self-appointed
'John Bull', occasionally being used as a kind of wobbly occasional table,
cradling an array of other people's half-empty glasses. I wasn't too
surprised to spot old Pat Pirbright hovering around the vol au vents
either, presumably gatecrashing to rub shoulders with his 'patriotic'
heroes. Around and between these gits swarmed a champagne-addled
orgy of tabloid-fed hatemongery, the sour cream bobbing on top of this
daft country's oceans of bile – a gunk which oils the gears of politics and
journalism and *real* elitism. The kind of self-appointed regressive
watchdogs who wait for any issue to arise – social equality of any kind,
social distancing, vaccination – and shackle themselves loudly to the *very
worst* side of any argument (which shouldn't even be an argument),
growing stronger with every single Like, every retweet, every talk show
spot, every angry response to their selfish muck-spreading. Any and every
response, in support or horrified opposition, to anything they barfed up
made these bigotry golems bigger and more successful, all feasting on the
hatred they received like bloated ticks. And no doubt every last twat of
them would probably claim to be taking on 'the elite'. The salt of the earth,
they thought themselves. Admittedly, they did make me desperate for a
drink.

The car programme guy was there, of course, the sagging faces of a few tabloid columnists I recognised from *Have I Got News For You*, plus the odd plug-ugly failed actor, and that one who was on *The Apprentice*, which thankfully I've never watched. I had always turned a blind eye to these people, and I tried very hard in the relative darkness of the disco-lit ballroom, but these leering, fag-end-dangling faces kept jumping out at me as I snarled my way from song to song. I could think of no array of faces I would rather see covered up, but obviously, every last homunculus there was maskless – some were even coughing extravagantly to huge roars of laughter – and all were soon gyrating together in the least socially distant manner imaginable.

The dear old Rev. Pinker-Byng was not one of those preachers prone to firing out fire and brimstone BS from the pulpit, but I was struck by something he once said about Hell which had somehow clung on to the sides of my brain: "*He will drink the wine of God's wrath, poured full strength into the cup of his anger, and he will be tormented with fire and sulphur as holy angels look on...*" and then there was something about a lamb. There generally was, I always just assumed he was really into lambs. Throw in the odd facial tattoo in gothic writing, the odd rictus face-job, and a hot and sweaty buffet, and you pretty much had the Hades which faced us poor daft balladeers that night.

The heating seemed to be set to 'Twentieth Level of Hell', and condensation was dripping down the ancient wallpaper, dropping off the nose of sundry dead animal heads. I openly admit that I myself was perspiring like a minor Royal on *Newsnight*, and no doubt my bandmates were similarly sweating cobs, buns, baps and rolls. Perhaps I should delete that earlier dig at Sam's sweatiness on this score, the fact that he's a budding fascist should be infamy enough.

Sweaty or not, however, we gave the hooting hot-pot of bastards the rockin', rollin', funky works – 'Johnny B Goode', 'The Girl Can't Help It', 'Twisting The Night Away', 'Superstitious', 'Let's Stay Together', 'Midnight Hour', 'What's Going On', 'Reach Out', 'Respect', 'Three Little Birds', 'Nutbush', 'Sex Machine', 'Hit The Road, Jack', 'My Girl', 'Dancing On the Ceiling', 'Foxy Lady' 'Little Red Corvette', 'Don't Turn Around', 'Red Light Spells Danger', 'Bad', 'Single Ladies', 'Happy'... the idea was ~~at~~ *that* at some point it might just dawn on at least one of the fascist little horde that every single song they'd been dancing and singing along to was written by a genius P.O.C. of some description, but it was obviously pointless. *"Celebrate, good times, come on!"* these flabby red-faced White Knights of the Barely United Kingdom hooted along, oblivious to any irony. I was tempted to see how far we could push it, and throw in 'Ebony & Ivory', but was outvoted, as that was mainly McCartney anyway.

The little drone whirred away above, below and around us, blasting out the biggest beats you could imagine from such a tiny woofer. Of course, pissed yobs did everything they could to try and catch the machine, but every time they made a lunge, Ziggy, back in the van, was adept enough to zoom up and out of the way, and keep his Dad's beat going.

Mein host was thankfully absent for much of the painful two hours of hot noise, but it was during the keytar break for Sly Stone's 'Dance To The Music' that a colossal roar went up, and there he was: Van Hurl, the anti-masker general, presumably fresh from yet another trolling appearance on *Newsnight*. That is, of course it was him, but despite this pointedly being advertised as a 'Maskless Ball' – us band-members aside – a spirit of fancy dress must have overtaken the Lord of the Manor, as he steamhammered his way into the creaking ballroom in full suit of armour, previously owned by one careful Medieval Lord Yaxley. All twenty-plus stone of Troy Van Hurl had somehow been folded into the ancient armour like a day-glo orange sofa crammed into a toilet cubicle, and his gruesome visage spilled out of the front of the helmet, smirkingly accepting this ovation from his bum-licking entourage. Worst of all, trailing there behind him, was Sam Blount, carrying what even in the darkness of the ballroom looked heart-stoppingly like a prototype of the IronCow special Silver edition vinyl doll and pencil case.

"Someone shut this bunch of fags up, will ya?" boomed Van Hurl, which was lucky, as the sight of said pencil case had caused my fingers to turn to melted marshmallow on the keys. The drone let out a derisory drum fill, and I could see Lotto and Neville edge towards their own wide open windows as the hubbub bubbled away, and the host began to talk. Or rather, to spew words.

"Proud boys and gentlemen, White knights and liberty-loving ladies, it's good to be back together, and it's GREAT to welcome you to my seat of power, to YAXLEY HALL, home of generations of blue-blooded bastions – yeah, I said bastions – of the ANGLO-SAXON nobility."

At this, drunken cheers of course went up. There was a lot more to it, but it's painful to even try to reconstruct. Stuff about Brexit, of course, about sunlit uplands and proud Britannia, stuff about freedom and winning world wars and powdered egg, as if anybody there had ever needed to taste the crap.

At one particularly snide line about "the woke zombies", Circular Sam seemed to cheer so hard, he froze in a kind of silent scream, emitting a tiny wail so high it was almost for dog's ears only. The look of orgasmic horror on his little mush suggested to me that, having clearly swiped the IronCow from my flat yesterday, the bent copper might have finally had enough electricity trickling over his brain-cell to have decided to open it up and see what was inside. His eyes rolled back, and he began to growl.

The IronCow flailed in his weak grip. If I just edged over to his side of the crowd while everyone was wrapt in their leader's blethering rhetoric, maybe I could grab my deadly bovine cartoon merchandise and leg it. But edging and legging it are both things much easier typed than done in a clumping forty-year-old prop space suit. Nonetheless, I was just agonising inches away from the IronCow when a particularly legless partygoer with a hundred thousand Twitter followers and stupendous mammaries falling out of her Stella McCartney emitted an "Ooh!" which drew a moment's pause from the torrent of oratory offal as she grabbed the IronCow from the oblivious Sam and cuddled it to herself with a screwed-up face and babygirl "Sowwy" to Van Hurl, who chuntered on, this time about how the evils of drugs were a genetic problem or some such, somehow linked to the evils of LGBTQ+ activism.

I tried to look inconspicuous, and strode over to the open patio door. Our band-link-up was still live, and I managed to whisper to Dobbin, "Pete, I've got this thing I have to do – can you get ready to play the emergency tape as soon as this nightmare effing BS is over? I want to go home!"

"10-4. Which means yeah!" he whispered back.

I don't know how long the whatever-number Earl of Yaxley had been bawling his crowd-pleasing bum-gravy, but he seemed to be reaching a crescendo. "Everybody's PROUD these days! God-damn Pride flags everywhere you look – good for business, what can ya do? But if that lot can be proud, what about us? Why should we not be PROUD to be Anglo-Saxon? All lives matter, don't they? If you tickle me, do I not chuckle? If you cut me, do I not bleed? Something which I do not suggest you try, by the way, I don't bleed easily, let me tell ya. If you suck me do I not – yadda, yadda, Shakespeare. This is OUR country, where we have lived for THOUSANDS of years, from here ANGLO-SAXONS have civilised the WORLD, and now we just gotta do the same for these GAY lovin', BLACK-power-knee-takin', drug-pushin' stupid SHEEPLE out there who gotta learn that ALL LIVES MATTER, BUT SOME LIVES ARE ALWAYS GONNA MATTER MORE!"

It was with immaculate good fortune that this final blast of bile caused such an eruption amongst the crowd that the J-list celeb with the IronCow threw her arms high up in the air, the precious pencil case with it. The IronCow's pocket was gaping open as it hurtled through the air, and I'm sure it wasn't a trick of the light that I saw a sizeable shower of small amber pellets of E.I.T.E. fall from its pocket and fizz into the punch. That might explain a lot about the scenes which greeted the emergency services later that night.

But I had no time to care for spiked punch, I was lost in the moment and with, I dare to say, a quite remarkable show of untapped sporting prowess, I zoomed forward and managed to catch the cow by the horn, and as our recorded performance of 'Standing In The Shadows Of Love' exploded out of the sound system, I almost barrel-rolled out into the fresh night air, and was enveloped by gorgeously cool darkness.

It was double darkness, of course, with my shades wedged on by my face mask and the helmet, which may have explained my somewhat random route towards the DD van, which saw me walking into some large trees of some furry description, and in a circle back to the side of the ballroom, desperately clutching the dodgy toy heifer. I dared to raise my helmet's visor and wriggled my face free of my mask.

Perhaps it was relief from this, and the sheer stark contrast to the hellhole within, but what a glorious evening it seemed to be, had any other event been taking place. It was an oddly balmy night, the shrubberies and flowers and whatnot were pumping out a whole rainbow of pleasing perfumes, sundry insects zooming about like nobody's business, the new moon blazing away in a starry sky, and had I been there just for a casual puff rather than a crucifying ordeal I may even have whistled something whimsical. I was almost tempted to reward myself with a J there and then, when a voice from the inky blackness took me entirely by surprise. Sometimes the light at the end of the tunnel is just someone lighting a brazier to broil your balls, and in a worst case scenario... I always prefer to be somewhere else.

"YO, WOKE-OH."

Of course, I dropped the IronCow. When everything has gone Pete Tong, but then gets worse, is that called 'gone Gary Davies'? I've forgotten to mention that the pencil case had a built-in IronCow security system, where the eyes flash red and it plays quotes from the show – "*Dat's an udder story!*" and "*Mooove along, now!*" and "*I got a gun – FRESIAN!*" This the novelty pencil case relentlessly proceeded to do, and I could see my assailant lunge for it... and then stop.

"Pick it up," he said.

"Why don't you pick it up?" I countered.

"This toy yours?"

"Yes, this is my priceless IronCow merchandise, thank you. I'll just be taking it and going down the hill to my home, thank you..." I wittered on, and reached down into the grass... and stopped. I may not exactly be

Mel-Smith-sized, but the suit simply refused to allow me to reach down any further than about a foot from the grass.

"What's in it?" he growled.

"Um... no idea at all about that, nope."

"But it's yours? Lemme see. We got a cop right here tonight, ya know."

The infamous pussy grabber grabbed at the air again, and I could see the skin-tight suit of armour was even more restrictive for him than my astronaut costume was for me.

We both lurched there, in the red-flashing darkness, each adversary equally incapable of bending over sufficiently to reach the prize. He stretched, and grunted, I reached, and yowled, and the IronCow mooed and wisecracked:

"*Don't hit a cow, man! – Moo! – Skip the bull! – Moo!*" And whatnot.

Suddenly, a rustle from some nearby foliage revealed two dishevelled figures – one was the gas-guzzling TV presenter, the other a blonde who I've since been assured was Julie Spode, ex-shock-journo and PR guru behind the launch of UKNews, the new flag-waving cartoon *Daily Mail* network watched by only the maddest minorities in Middlesex. Both wore blushes lit by mobile phone glow.

"Oh, your Lordship!" simpered the latter, wrenching her dress out of some complicated aperture or other. "What a simply ripping party, thank you."

"She means, a stirring protest, Troy, a stirring protest. Is everything...?"

"Can you grab me that goddamn flashing chicken thing there on the ground?"

"Oh, of course," she beamed, grabbing the IronCow and stuffing it firmly into Van Hurl's gauntlets. "Isn't it a cow?"

"Anyway, yes," harrumphed he, "We'd better be getting our coats. I mean, I'll be getting *my* coat..."

"And I'll be getting my own coat. Separately."

"Whatever," grinned the victorious Van Hurl.

"... And, er, leave you both to it. Thanks for the party, old boy!"

"And, um, up the White Knights!"

They slinked, slunk, or slank off, leaving open a door which shed just that bit more unwelcome light on our own little tangle.

"You remember what I said I was gonna do with you if I found you sniffing round this castle again? Like a seagull to a McDonalds trashcan, ain't ya? Drugs..." Van Hurl had hold of the IronCow's chunky zipper, and was enjoying his moment, slowly opening the case. "You know why I hold no truck with drugs?"

"*Let's take the bull by the horns, man!*"

"Look, neither do I, honestly, it's just not..."

"Shush your mouth now, Woke-Oh. You say this is your faggot cow bag. What you been dealing here at this exclusive party tonight, huh?" He raised a gigantic metallic arm, and prodded me in the chest, while sharing some particularly libellous views about my parenthood and appearance. From the depths of my space suit, Suri interjected:

146

*"Okay, I found this on the web for, 'Abbatoirs'! Check it out..."*

By the time I had silenced Suri with a deft slap, Van Hurl had fished out the torn baggie of Irn-Bru-like amber pellets, and they glinted in the half-light, seeming to make the White Knight's piggy eyes flash amber under his helmet.

*"Looks like we won't be livin' happy heifer after!"*

"You wanna know why I hate this kinda shit? I'll tell you, as you're about to have your head popped off like a tube of Pringles. I hate drugs, because I done it all, boy. I snorted lines off the desk at the Oval Office, I had uppers, downers, bend-you-rounders. I was the guy who gave John Belushi his last speedball, man, and you know what? They ain't never done SHIT for me..."

*"What's the beef, baby?"*

"And you wanna know why? Because I got BLUE BLOOD, man! I'm super. I ain't just any old race, I'm Anglo-Saxon royalty! It's gonna take a whole Afghanistan of poppies to floor Troy Van Hurl!"

In the murk, I could see him push a fistful of E.I.T.E. into his mouth, his shining white teeth mashing the tabs into orangey mush which continued to glint in the half-light. He paused, and swallowed.

"See? Candy for bullshit kids, and you come here peddling this crap at MY party? What did I say I was gonna do to you if I caught you stinkin' up my realm, boy? I'm gonna put my knee on your bitch neck until you can't breath no more!"

It all spilled over. "Boy" may have been the trigger. I'm a man of peace, not a social warrior. But something twanged in my brain, and suddenly Minnie was streaking through the air and colliding with an almighty THUNK-BOOF in the messed-up visage of Troy Van Hurl's hallucinogen-grinding face.

I fell to the ground, still clutching dear old Millie, who was dropping precious keys all over the grass. Blood was beginning to spout from behind Van Hurl's horrendous visor. His grin was massive, and haunting.

"So you do have some spunk in you, Banjo! And I'm-a-gonna whip every pint of that spunk out of ya, an' squeeze out your cockamamie shit-eatin' woke-oh virtue-signallin', goddamn mask-wearin' homosexual innards an' make you play them bum boy tubes like a harmonica. I'm a-gonna pull your spine out through your lil wang an' floss your teeth with it!"

"Now, come on, that seems a bit..."

*"Pull de udder one!"*

"'Cause yo' bad news, boy, yo' FAKE news, an' I AM THE MOTHER-KICKIN' EARLDOOK O'YAXLEY! AN' I AM A *WHITE KNIIIIIGHT*!!"

The urgency of the moment gave me some extra swing, enough to launch myself out into the blackness, broken Minnie tumbling who knows where, and off downhill as fast as my astronaut's legs could take me. I heard the scream of His So-Called Lordship's charge near behind me, a stream of booming oaths of racial hatred... and I ran as I never thought possible in the clothes of Mel Smith. I don't know if you've ever tried to outrun an articulated lorry going downhill at 500 miles per hour, but I honestly don't recommend it. Down, down, down in the darkness the two of us windmilled, until at last I managed to somehow bounce myself off to the side, landing in some handy fuzzy oversized thicket, thankfully saved from a thousand nettle stings and thistle prongs by the space suit's padding.

It was pitch black. I just stayed completely still, and didn't even breathe. It seemed the least I could do. I just kept waiting, holding my breath, for what seemed several months, determined to keep my location entirely to myself. Only after what seemed to be another fortnight did I dare to relax a little, and I lit up a trembling J to steady my shredded nerves.

/

## Chapter Eleven

There's really nothing worse than a nadir. As far as the space suit allowed,
I balled myself up foetally, eyes screwed tight, and hoped that I wasn't
about to be splatted into paté by a drug-crazed madman in Medieval fancy
dress. What a way to go that would have been. After surely several days of
this, sprawled there as I was in the darkness and indeed scratchy
stingy-ness, a slowly apparent whirring sound out of the black
temporarily befuddled me, until the winking red eye of the Mulliner drone
announced its presence.

"There you are, Banjo," Pete's tinny voice came over a small built-in
speaker. "Am I on speaker, Zig? Good. For Freddie bloody Mercury's sake,
man, what are you playing at? We're all packed up, run round the front
and jump in the van, we're getting out of this frickin' Nazi bunker."

Then Neville's voice: "And Lotto's got the full payment, shag!
WOO-HOO!"

The drone veered off away from the prickly thicket, and away from the
house, and by following its graceful path, I managed to locate my
bandmates, and bundle myself in the van.

"Home, Dobbin, and don't spare the – things that you don't spare to go
fast..." Not classic wit from me, I know, but I was still thumping with
adrenaline.

I explained to my fellow drones what had taken place as far as I
understood it. The idea of what a deranged Van Hurl would do with the

IronCow and the E.I.T.E. in its udder pocket, I wobbled to imagine, but I was advised by all to keep a low profile for a while. Easy enough for a guy to do under lockdown, maybe, but the following day's news made their advice all the more urgent.

My sleep had been far from dreamless, with long sweaty bouts of trying to fend off monstrous tin cans overflowing with sewage. It was something to do with making a pop video for Barry White's comeback or something, but calm down, I'm finished with the dream recall now.

I eventually awoke with intense need for caffeination, and pulled on my louchest pyjamas in the heliotrope shade, bunged on an old *Pop Somebodies* beanie, and flopped to the kitchen, making a special effort to avoid the news from any portal, when the text arrived from Lotto:

'Shit. Man. This. Is. WONDERFUL. And we got paid in advance! woot!' Plus they attached a link to the *Guardian* article: "VAN HURL FOUND DEAD IN BOG." "Bit of a *Sun* headline for them," I was just thinking, when the actual meaning of the words fell on me from a tall height.

It's very difficult with moments like this, to decide how much obvious terrain to trudge over, when at least half the country remembers this story breaking – the colossal cheers from the 48% and more planned piss-ups to celebrate than there had been since Thatcher fell off the perch and into the guano, and of course, the endless twisted conspiracy theorising and threats of angry reprisals from the scariest of the other lot. Golf-haters were particularly targeted by the outraged Van Hurl fans, apparently.

As reported on that first day, the facts were that Troy Van Hurl, having staged an illegal anti-masker event at Yaxley Castle, attending in fancy dress in full Medieval armour, had got into a fight and then somehow hurled himself down the hill and tumbled into the old Yaxley bog, and been unable to extricate himself as the thick gloopy mud oozed through the visor. It was only as the narrative developed and tests were carried out, that it was revealed that he was utterly off his bone-head bonce on some unfamiliar new hallucinogenic drug, which came to be labelled 'ODD E' by the press. "Outrageous!" the racist faithful responded all over the media, "When Van Hurl was always preaching against drugs? He must have been spiked!"

But there was a loony ambivalence, too, about the absurd death of such an absurd bogeyman. Panel games roared at it without delay, contestants overjoyed not to have to think up any new material, out-gunned by reality once again. Even all but the most secretly Nazi newsreaders always seemed to have smirks ghosting over their lips when the updates came around. To most of Van Hurl's inner-circle, it seemed like the Wicked Witch's legs were sticking out from under their house, and they were finally free to dish every last scrap of dirt about the corporation's inner workings – and the endless narcotics, legal and illegal, scooped up like popcorn by the deceased boss. His kids now had full control of the US business – hotels, casinos, endless golf courses – and seemed as happy to put their lucky bereavement down to 'misadventure' as... well, of course, as I was.

The problem is, truth bombs seem to have only the tiniest impact these days, the general line being 'Yes, we know everyone with power is lying all the time, but we're playing the game here, don't spoil it with the truth or we will pointedly ignore you, if you're lucky.' And so, it's scary to imagine what some twisted trolls still believe really happened at Yaxley Castle that night.

With the news fresh in my barely caffeinated mind, it was hard to know what to freak out about first. Some kind of organised Freak Out To Do List needed to be formulated, and I tried to juggle them about.

I, Banjo Wajih Wako, am no killer.

Even if the target was by far the smelliest skunk on the street, you wouldn't hire me to wipe anybody out, any more than you would headhunt Marilyn Manson to be your babysitter. I struck a blow, I know, but I never forced his head under the muck! But then, if my name should come up in piggy circles, would there be any way to prove it? I had failed to return home with the IronCow bursting with massively incriminating sweeties, and worst of all, poor Minnie was lying up there somewhere, bloodied and brutalised.

I decided I may as well just have a nice hot shower, put on my best eye-popping ensemble, and await the buzz of the fuzz at my front door. That Morning After couldn't have been more depressing if the shade of The Spirit of Xmas Yet To Come was drifting towards me looking extra-specially apologetic.

Before I could disrobe there was a buzz, though, and I went to answer the door with something of the impressive sobriety of a French nob stepping up to the guillotine. In the walkway, at admirable social distance, stood JJ, cradling a preposterously large double bass case. She opened it to reveal that bastard IronCow – and my darling Minnie.

"I believe I have managed to retrieve all of the missing keys, and wiped most of the blood off them," she said.

"Oh my satanic aunt, Minnie! JJ! Thank the non-existent Jah it's you! Do you think we're being watched?"

"I apologise that my knowledge of police procedure is not expansive, but I fancy the contingency to be logically unlikely, Banjo. I surmised, however, that you would be in a state of considerable agitation, given the events of the previous evening."

"You can repeat that an infinite amount of times, yes. I believe I may be somewhere neck-deep in the bum liquid."

"I hesitate to say 'I told you so', but... I did furnish you with an accurate prediction of events. It was a case of singular good fortune that I was able to speed selectively up the A49, and secrete myself in the environs of the Ballroom verandah before the evening's conclusion."

"Smokey's sweet sandals, JJ, you mean you were actually *there*?"

"Naturally – how else would I have been able to rescue your keytar, and make away with the IronCow novelty pencil case?"

I must have stammered something particularly gasp-packed and unintelligible, as she continued:

154

"Every trace of E.I.T.E. has already been... destroyed. I will simply have to save my research for some less sensitive juncture. But I thought you might like your toy back?"

I ogled the troublesome little faux-metallic moo-cow. "I don't think I want this anywhere near me, JJ, who knows who's still looking for it?"

"I had considered whether this may be the cause of some perturbation, Banjo."

"Tell you what, I'll give it to my Uncle Tim. It's fake, I know, but a pretty rare fake, so should make up for the state of the old space suit he lent me. And my Uncle Tim is an absolute connoisseur of any old cack."

I had a fiddle with Minnie, and even given the missing keys it was clear something was not right with her internal workings.

"Oh, poor Min, poor Min, poor Min!" I crooned. "But I'm pretty sure there's nothing wrong here Lotto wouldn't be able to tinker into submission. Don't you worry, Minnie. You'll be safer with Auntie... Uncle... with Lotto, for a while, anyway." I turned to my saviour. "JJ, I really don't know how to repay you for this. I awoke thinking my day was certain to end in an unfashionably grey small room with a toilet in it, but now some slight rhythm of hope begins to tick away like a jazzy hi-hat just waiting for a bassline. You're something of a marvel."

"Not at all, Banjo, I have to confess, I hadn't calculated for half of last night's events to unfold as they did, but I think we can be confident of no unfair reprisals coming our way."

"I know it all seems a bit 'Ding dong, the bastard's dead', but I wasn't exactly setting out to inspire him to charge into a face full of deadly bog matter! I can't help feeling a little... erm... Not sad, exactly, but..."

"Perhaps 'culpable' would be the *mot juste*? You logically cannot lay any meaningful blame for such imponderable developments upon yourself, Banjo, any more than you could applaud yourself. Some individuals are perhaps simply headed for calamity. 'The stroke of death is as a lover's pinch, which hurts and is desired.'"

"Ooh, that's good, could I use it as a lyric?"

"If you wish, I believe the Bard of Avon's copyright ran out some years ago."

"Ah, him again! Thanks, though, honestly. I only wish I could reward you with gold and peacocks and precious whatevers for this glorious intervention."

"Please, stop, Banjo, it was the obvious course of action."

"Just let me know if I can ever do anything, though?"

"Well, as you seem so insistent, hmmm... you could lose the beanie, perhaps, if you'll forgive me saying so, it doesn't suit you."

I laughed. The beanie was rather gross, but had been with me for eons.

"No, you're right, it's revolting." I removed the scummy hat, and twanged it off into the wide blue yonder, crying, "Begone, noughties throwback!"

I'm sure the distant relative of a smile flickered over JJ's lips, and I was beginning to wonder how I might turn it into a laugh, when my laptop butted in with a 'ping':

"*You have a new message in – Drones chat – from – Dobbin.*"

"Gah, why the frick is my computer designed to annoy me so much?" I asked myself, stepping inside to check the source of the pinging, and grumbling as I went. "Why did I click all the speech activation options? The brief thrill of feeling like a *Star Trek* captain talking to the bridge evaporated within minutes. I'll have to get Lotto to fix the damn thing along with poor Minnie..."

But when I returned to the door, JJ had somehow managed to evaporate, without so much as a puff of smoke. Strange, her mother was always a fan of the French exit too. I shrugged, and turned to the chat – between us, I was sure the Dinham Drones would just about escape with whatever integrity we had intact, and my pals would have my back. They say a problem shared is a problem halved. So logically, if you loudly tell your problem to EVERYONE, it must be almost totally solved.

Pete had kicked off a group chat between us, with a smudgy-looking video, and both Lotto and Neville were responding with excited GIFs of all kinds when I began to take it in.

The video was clearly drone footage, in some kind of night vision. A big white blobby thing was hitting a big black and orange thing with something heavy, and then the latter thing began to chase the blobby thing down the hill, sloping away from the major light source. After thirty seconds or so of pursuit, the blobby thing bounced off into dark undergrowth, while the black and orangey thing seemed to pick up speed in the original direction. The drone followed the speeding black and orange thing for half a minute or so, before returning to check on the blobby thing – alerted by a great plume of smoke curling up from the bushes.

How that eternity of breath-holding survival could have flashed by in less than a couple of minutes of drone footage I do not understand, but then technology really beats me sometimes, as you might have guessed. But there was the truth – admittedly in a blocky sort of Minecrafty simplicity, but Pete was sure it would be useful proof if any of us happened to be dragged into the sordid investigation.

Neville: 'BUT SHAGS THERE'S JUST 8,637,927,283,028,902,183,393,932,661,759 THINGS I STILL DON'T UNDERSTAND.'

Pete: 'I SAY IT GETS YOU OFF ANY HOOK MATE. I'VE HALF A MIND TO SEND THE VID TO THE FILTH RIGHT AWAY, SAY I'M JUST A LOCAL BREWER WHO WAS SHOWING HIS SON HOW TO FLY THE DRONE & WE CAUGHT THIS BIT OF FOOTAGE'

Lotto: 'BUT WHY GET US INVOLVED AT ALL? LET'S JUST KEEP SCHTUM OR IS IT SHTUM AND RIDE IT OUT'

Me: 'SHTOOM?'

Lotto: 'EXACTLY.'

Neville: 'THERE'S ONE THING OF WHICH I AM ABSOLUTELY CERTAIN. I JUST WISH I KNEW WHAT IT WAS.' (Smiley with a tongue waggling.)

Me: 'COMMITTING MURDER IS THE MOST HIDEOUSLY EMBARRASSING THING I HAVE EVER DONE. AND I DID TALENT TV! ... SHIT NOW I SAID I COMMITTED MURDER AND THIS WILL END UP BEING READ OUT IN COURT WON'T IT?'

Lotto: 'BANJO YOU DID NOT COMMIT MURDER. THAT'S LIKE BLAMING THIS VIRUS ON A POOR BAT BEING BUGGERED IN SOME STEAMY WET MARKET'

Pete: 'YOU STRUCK A BLOW, MAN!'

Lotto: 'IT WAS A HEAD FULL OF POISON AND VEINS FULL OF MUTANT UPPERS WHICH PEGGED THE SHITTER'

Neville: 'YEAH WHAT THEY JUST SAID SHAG TOTALLY. CHILL BANJO'

Pete: 'THEY WILL NEVER FIND THOSE DASTARDLY DING-DANG-DONGS!'

But chill I could not. I threw a wobbly that night, and throwing wobblies has never been part of my nature. It seems to me that if you throw wobblies, you should be prepared to go and pick them up again. I considered once again just walking in to the Police station and declaring my involvement, but to my knowledge there's no Dinham CID, so that would have meant a journey to Kidderminster or somewhere, so I thought again.

And again, and again – there was little else to do that lockdown summer, and I slipped on my new pair of Sungod Vulcans which some guy in a club in Hereford swore were once owned by Nile Rogers, and stretched out on my musical bower – by which I mean, a sun lounger out on the flat front porch-walkway, surrounded by Auntie Akifa's rhododendrons – and I replayed the events of that dire disco, over and over, strumming mindless chords to songs that would never be worth remembering, deaf to the banging from neighbours. I started to piece together something called 'Millennial Lament', but then I went to the bathroom mirror, took a good look at my face, slapped it a few times, and stopped.

With no pubs to perform in, no festivals to play at, the warm days just burbled along, the fresh wodge in my bank account bringing little joy to the doldrums. Texts remained unanswered, doorbells rang on deaf ears. I couldn't even be bothered to shrug.

Things worsened when the Mulliner household had a visit from the West Mercia Constabulary. Pete's van had been spotted at Yaxley Castle on the night in question, and he happily and helpfully gave up his drone footage without demur, whatever tales he span of his presence that night giving the law the confidence to let him go after only a couple of hours of questioning, stopping short his *Line Of Duty* fantasies with disappointing formality. He was lucky to escape the £1,000 fine for breaking lockdown rules, at least. The WMC were probably glad to just have all those anecdotes about the recording of Slade's third album out of earshot.

Blow my bits, this story has become positively Goth, hasn't it? I have always tried to maintain a spirit of happy-go-lucky, it's just that some periods turn out a bit more gloomy-cum-doomed. Things will cheer up soon – I give you my solemn promise.

Neverthefewer, in those familiar doldrums, as I continued to await that knock on the door I brooded, and I plucked and plonked, and croaked and smoked. One such stuffy afternoon I had closed my eyes out on the bower, and was just attempting to meditate when I felt two hands clasped over my face.

"Guess what?!"

"Don't you mean 'who'?" I tried to say, but Poppy was unstoppable, grabbing my head in a vice-like grip and somehow managing to laugh like a fun fair sailor at the same time as clamping her mouth on mine. I don't know if you've ever been to the dentist, sitting there with your mouth wide open, and had them suddenly fall in, but the sensation must be similar.

"I'm back, my faerie lad!" she grinned as soon as our mouths had autonomy.

"WHAT A FANTASTIC SURPRISE!" I did my best to beam, and it probably came out as more of a goggle.

"Yes, darling one, I got bored of breathing the clean air of Glossop's ages ago, the place is becoming a bit run down to be honest, so I got Honoria and Pocoyo to come and pick me up. I've been staying with them in their yurt since Thursday."

Presumably I was supposed to have some idea who this Honoria and Pocoyo were, maybe due to some kind of osmosis, but as ever, I had no gap to reflect with Poppy, as I was shooting down another waterslide of tumbling sweet and sour nothings.

"Isn't it simply gorgeous news about the defeat of the nasty old bog monster?" she crowed. "I swear, when Dad and I were cleaning up at the castle I was just one sweaty grope away from the out-of-court settlement of a lifetime! Bad man gone – good." And she kissed me again.

I had tried to hide any tremor of emotion at the mention of Van Hurl, and thankfully the conversation veered once again.

"Though for all the nasty things he came out with, Van Hurl was a bit of a stopped clock when it comes to this pandemic hoax. I bet you're still wearing a mask and everything," she said, eyes a-rolling, and I sighed. Poppy had found another wrong end of a stick to cling onto. "Why on Gaia's sweet Earth would anyone trust a word this government has to say about anything, Banjo? The whole virus thing is a joke, they just want to keep THE PEOPLE away from each other, to stop LOVE blooming wherever it would go, it's a conspiracy against the sheeple!"

I probably mumbled something about being better safe than sorry, or best of all, neither. What I wanted to say was that only bothering to take issue with the crooked billionaires running the show over all these basic medical precautions was like a little mouse looking up at a fat cat licking its lips, and fretting that puss was spiking its cheese. But shtum I remained, I somehow let all that argument fuel drain away, and looked at

Poppy. She was looking suitably scrubbed up after her latest chemical adventure, her hair this time a blaze of auburn and lilac. As ever, the view was one it was very difficult not to admire.

"Awww, I feel I've been neglecting my big Banjo bear," she eventually said.

"Oh no, no, don't worry about that at all," I said, and decided to offer her a drink. I wanted one myself, and perhaps the days of solitude were sending me a bit barmy. And she had come all this way. Display basic manners? It would be rude not to.

"JJ explained about your need for a good bit of rest, I hope you got it."

"That was very naughty of Jemima not to keep my little secret," Poppy replied, "And I guessed that my Daddy Bear would instantly return all of her fantastic mind-blowing brain candy, like the big boy scout that you are. Yes, rehab was rehabilitating, thank you. But how can I ever keep secrets from you anyway, Banjo-bear? We are engaged, after all."

I let out an elongated chuckle that I suppose in some dimension or other could have been taken as a sound of agreement. That must have been the dimension which Poppy came from. "I should probably, like, leave some of my stuff here, you know? Toothbrush, tarot deck, just the essentials. I know how easily spooked you are by womanly attentions, you typical toxic straight male!"

"Poppy, what do you take me for?" I replied.

"Because you're there," she grinned.

I cluck-chuckled some more, with perhaps an extra shade of drowning goose thrown into the mix, and Poppy joined in as gin and cherryade fizzed in two glasses. I urged myself: here I was, in this apparently inescapable situation, maybe it was finally time to give Poppy a proper chance, at last? I was certainly running out of excuses for my aunties as to why I'm still single – I was thinking that when the topic arises at the next Christmas dinner, I might just lay all the blame on Cotton-Eye Joe. Perhaps I have been on the shelf too long – the brackets are going to give way. Plus, I tried telling myself, better the devil you know... but the reply came back, sometimes it is worth the effort to get out and meet new devils.

I hadn't felt myself for quite some days, and misery loves company. At least for a while, then it becomes insouciance, and wants to be alone again. So as there just didn't seem any honourable way of exorcising my home of Pirbrights, and Poppy seemed here to stay, I began to stream a box set of epic TV for us both, and hoped for the best.

I remember her taking a spare moment between asphyxiating embraces to threaten me: "We should go travelling together, Banjo. I want to spend six months travelling India. And I want a baby."

I blinked. "Before, after or during?" But then there was no more talking.

I won't just draw a veil over the rest of the evening, I insist on wrapping it securely in thick bubble wrap, and a chunky blanket, before securing the flaps with strong duct tape. Suffice it to say, I should hope, that Poppy was still 100% a fixture in my domain two mornings later, and I was running out of excuses to pop to the shops for breathing space.

It was a hot and sunny noon when I arose with a "Hey hey" to find her licking gingerly at what looked like a snotty tissue. There in a scrap of white paper bag were the orangey remnants of three or four of JJ's experimental sweeties.

I said nothing, but the look on my face must have betrayed enough to trigger any number of possible narratives in the Pirbright cranium, because she laughed, "Oh, oopsie doodle! Naughty Poppy! Bahahaha! Come on, Banjo, you're a big boy now, why don't you try one? Aren't you ever a little curious? Curiosity allowed the cat to become informed and make its own deductions. But THEY want you to think he's dead. Man. Go on... a little Ecstasy In The Evening, no...?"

"Poppy, it's not even 1p.m."

"The look on your face! What's it got to do with you, these sweeties? It's not as if the Gestapo Pigs are going to crash in here and arrest us, is it?"

Not for the first time, I gazed into Poppy's eyes, and felt the need to tell her all about the Ding Dang Dong disaster, my part in Van Hurl's downfall, and the affair of the E.I.T.E. and the IronCow. But the sheer weight of experience I had racked up, of what happened when Poppy Pirbright is given access to any kind of sensitive information, and the bizarre leaps of bad logic she was prone to make given any stimulus, stopped me dead in my tracks. This was the sad thing, the reason I needed to escape from whatever romantic entanglement I found myself in – I wanted to respect

Poppy, but I knew her. Confiding in her was like scratching your name and PIN Number into a bus stop. And so I just said, "It's not my kind of thing, Poppy. But that stuff especially is dodgy as a dog-do jammy dodger, that's all I'm saying."

"Oh GOD, you're just like my Dad!" And so a one-woman performance played out before me, "No, look, fine, I'm flushing them down the toilet, look, here I go! In fact, no, screw you, Banjo, you don't get to decide what goes in or out of my body, my body is a temple and I like to decorate it with all sorts of exciting exotic... things, and... this is getting too intense, I'm sorry, darling, but I'm going to meet Shaggy and Pocoyo for the evening and try to, like, realign my... my..."

"Self?" I offered. "Realign yourself."

"Chakras! Silly billy Banjo," she pouted, secreting the dodgy substances back in her Peruvian knapsack. "You will be fine without me for a while, won't you? I'll be back."

She clasped my face between her lips, and skipped off down the road. I couldn't help myself shouting after her, "Be careful! I'm here if you need me!" And then, a little quieter, "But only in those very specific circumstances. 24 seconds a day, 7 days of the year."

One thing Poppy's unexpected residence had stymied in me was any peace in which to play some music, so I took Minnie outside, and tried to find some inspiration in the blue-skied sunshine – killing me S with my S's – and still with zero sign of musical breakthrough.

It was in this melodically constipated mode that I was eventually drawn to the sight of a string bean of a cyclist dismounting before Wickham Mansions and wiping perspiration from his de-helmeted brow as he approached my own doorstep. Summer had almost given up, but it was muggy in the extreme. He looked down at where I was plonking disconsolately at my freshly rewired and re-keyed muse.

"Gosh, It is, it is you, isn't it? Banjo Wako?" grinned the visitor. "You know, your second album, *Liking It Like,* got me through the worst of Hendon back in the day. I can't believe it's you, here in Dinham."

"Pleasure!" I piped up, not hugely used to the sudden appearance of fans, as I had been several years previously. "You can be sure it was a pleasure to bring any scrap of comfort to a blighted life, believe me, matey. Um, very happy to sign anything you want besmirched with my scribble and all that shizz."

This was the first ray of sunshine to beam down into the Wako zone for what felt like a geological period. I was all smiles as he produced a CD of the said album – that woebegotten cover with the snow leopard and the custard pie doing little to bum my buzz – and I poised the proffered Sharpie.

"Who's it to, my dear dude?"

"Detective Inspector Sandy Masood, West Mercian Police." He replied, and I froze as if tasered. I looked up at this young stripling, smiling a broad smile and pushing back a schoolboy spike of gelled hair. "Sorry, that was a bit *Midsomer Murders* of me, wasn't it?" He actually laughed, while I still felt my innards plunging towards the Earth's core at unstoppable speed, and flicked an aromatic J at my elbow into the rhododendrons. "Do you mind if I perch here?" He gestured towards Auntie Akifa's deckchair. Thank frick she was over at her friend Phyllis' house, cleaning her out at Black Jack.

I proffered the bum space. "Um, should you be wearing a mask, or...?"

"No, we're outside, it's quite breezy. Now the vaccines are rolling out, things have to improve, don't they? Ah..." He seemed to need the sit down. "Bliss. Now, look, I'm strictly off-duty here, sir, but you seem like a chap who can be trusted. So, that said, strictly *entrés nous*, or between us if you prefer... did you kill Troy Van Hurl?"

The three or four seconds of thespian craft required from me to phrase a reply were, I must admit, exhilarating. I felt like all the Sir Ians and Sir Patricks rolled into one. But the truth escaped my lips before my brain could trip myself up.

"No. No, I did not."

"No, you didn't, Banjo, if I may call you Banjo, Mr. Wako, you didn't – as far as I am aware and could possibly imagine – you did not kill anyone. I'm here in response to a concerned pillar of the community, shall we say, we have a mutual friend, who told me they are concerned about you, and I want you to be entirely reassured that the Van Hurl investigation has absolutely no intention of dragging you into the interview room. You see this?"

His tablet was paused at just the right moment in Pete's drone footage –
a round figure lashed out with a black stump of an object and hit the
J-peggy form of Van Hurl... and we know the rest.

"The autopsies have shown that this altercation had no bearing on the
cause of death, which was asphyxiation in mud, a result of the voluntary
ingestion of an unidentified synthetic hallucinogen. You don't do drugs, do
you, Banjo?"

I shamed myself with an antsy glance at the overflowing ashtray near
me – if that was 'drugs', then so was whisky, or creme eggs. Thankfully, my
visitor continued, oblivious.

"I remember you saying in that *NME* interview, July 2011, wasn't it?"

I shuddered. That candid chat about the delights of the grape and the
grain and the pleasingly feathery bush had earned me some of my most
bastardly brickbats, not least from Auntie Akifa, who still refers to the
affair as 'That Enemy You Talked With'.

"No, sir, I don't do any kind of drugs, it's simply not my scene."

"Exactly. Just doesn't compute." The cycling copper beamed again, and
apologetically mimed the need for a selfie. I tried to master the emotions
behind my mask of grins as he put his arm around me. "I can't believe it,
Banjo Wako!"

"So, am I free to go?"

"From your own home? You're free to do whatever you like, any old
time, Mr. Wako! Can you imagine, if we were to drag you into this case,
what the media would say? No way on Planet Earth you're going to be put

under that spotlight, my dear chap. As I say, I'm just here to settle a few silly qualms, and get the entire picture clear. At the risk of sounding all Poirot on a snowy train, you see, so many people wanted Troy Van Hurl dead. Dead, dead, and never called me mother. Sorry, I'm gabbling now."

"Gabble away, Detective Ins..."

"Sandy."

"Please gabble, Sandy."

"His kids have already taken control of Van Hurl Enterprises..."

"Frig it, I bet that gawky kid of his is going to turn up demanding his castle too..."

"I really couldn't say. The remains of the deceased have been discharged and shipped to Johannesburg as per his wishes. And... the conspiracy theorists continue to..."

"To theoretically conspire?"

"Actually, I was going to say 'conspiratorially theorise', but either will do. Despite capturing his penultimate moments alive, this drone footage is as inadmissible as it is irrelevant. There has already been one confession, you know? A former special police constable, member of the White Knight outfit, suddenly strides into the station claiming to be Van Hurl's killer, screaming about metal cows and killing for love."

I had heard the news – a week or two earlier, Sam Blount had wandered naked into the local Budgens, shouting that he was Judas and had murdered Van Hurl because the frigger was Jesus. Nobody believed him. It does take all sorts – even if some sorts would do best under heavy security surveillance.

"...The man in question is now getting the very best psychiatric care. He claimed that he was that round figure in the video, but as it happens, the case is closed. Misadventure. A risk that was taken voluntarily. Not murder, no matter how juicy the papers want the story to be. He was out of his mind, and hurled himself into a bog. We will of course be keeping an eye out for any dangerous substances in the region, similar to the chemicals discovered in Mr Van Hurl's system..."

"Bill Oddie or something, aren't they calling it?"

"There's already so much bizarre misinformation out there, but if they're still on the street, they're anything but Goodies. But otherwise, this can of worms can remain safely on the shelf. Oh, and just something like 'To Sandy' would be fine, thank you. Banjo Wako!" He grinningly shook his head again.

I was smacked out of my reverie, and gladly signed a fulsome autograph on the CD case. "And anything else you ever want me to sign, or selfies, or you know, I have some exclusive vinyl pressings here I could sign for you..."

"Oh, bribery!" he brayed like a donkey – but when he saw the look of fear dart back into my eyes, stopped abruptly. "No, honestly, that would be – beyond awesome, thank you. Your stuff has just always cheered me up, it's a great honour to have not-at-all-officially interviewed you."

So there we have it – no matter what the *Bhagavad Gita* reckons, what goes around, sometimes just stays there. DI Sandy Masood went off happily on his bicycle, and I finally felt that I could open my curtains without some kind of SWAT team or media scrum there waiting for me to spill the beans. These are my beans, to spill how I wish.

Opting for an early night, I gratefully slept the slumber of the innocent, at last, after so many sweaty and paranoid nights of duvet origami. I slept deep, and dreamlessly...

Until awoken by a phone call at 3 a.m. from someone who required no glance at the screen to identify.

"Ugh, 'lo?"

"BANJO, YOU BUGGERING BASTARD-BASHER! WERE YOU SLEEPING? LAZY GIT. I HAVE GREAT NEWS, MY DARLING IDLE YOUNG WASTREL NEPHEW! GET OUT OF BED! YOU'RE GOING TO THAT LONDON!"

## Chapter Twelve

"Er, what?"

"NOW!"

"Not when, I said 'what'?"

"There's no time for your babbling time wasting, young Banjo, it's time to stir yourself, the honour of our family demands it! What are you doing idling in bed at this hour? I imagined you down in some speakeasy hoovering up absinthe."

"It's Sunday night, Auntie Faiza..."

"WRONG! It's Monday morning, and you've got to get to London. And you have to stop an auction."

I sat there in the darkness and felt my brain trying to grab onto some semblances of rationality.

"Auntie, you haven't been snooping around this druggy story and been spiked by some dodgy Dudley dealer have you?"

"Of course not, you young tit, I'm as sober as the accused. But I've been on a long Zoom call with your employer."

"Mrs. J?" I knew the two matriarchs had long been members of a mutual appreciation society, but hadn't suspected that knocking back chablis till the small hours on video cam was their thing.

"Well of course Heather, you dear dipstick. And she had been talking to their ladyships up at the castle, and found that some of their dearest objet d'art had been shifted out by Van Hurl..."

"Spit, obviously", we chorused together.

"...And though most of it had been tracked down by the estate lawyers, one final lot has been irreversibly slated for auction in a London auction house at 9 o'clock in the morning."

"So, drop them an email!"

"Banjo, that's just not how the auction business works." It's testament to how deep-fried my grey matter was at that hour that this slipped by unquestioned. "The estate has contacted the auction house, but by the time anyone has seen any email, the priceless heirloom could already be halfway to Texas."

"Texas?"

"Or wherever art tycoons live these days. So it has to be in person. You couldn't prove ownership over the phone."

"Well, you'll enjoy the Monday morning drive down the M40, then."

"Lippy, Banjo! There's no way I could leave the house – Viv's tested positive."

"Oh no, what? How is she?"

"Rest assured, you greedy oinker, she's fine, that's what takes all the piss in the whole wide world. She's fine, we're fine, but we're confined to the grounds for fourteen days."

"Well if you ask me," I reasoned, "You should ask someone else."

"It has to be you, Banjo."

"But surely Mrs. J could..."

"Are you a Wako? Could you stand to send a grand lady of retirement vintage out into a cold Monday morning motorway? Your name was suggested, as it happens, by Lady Angela and Lady Bobbie – in unison, going by Heather's version of events. You've found yourself a couple of new fans there, my boy, blue blood twins, eh?" Auntie Faiza laughed fit to level the world's buildings to their foundations. "Heather agreed with them, that although it might seem a bit drastic to zoom out without delay to stop the auction, if anyone could do it, you were the man. They all agreed that you had the heart and the balls to step up to the plate when there was a good deed to be done. That sounds like the boy I helped to bring up."

"In the name of Hendrix, quite a conspiracy of matriarchs at work here, then!" I lightly fumed. "The next thing you'll tell me my arm's also being bended by..."

On cue, a banging at the connecting door. "BANJO, BOY! OPEN UP THIS DOOR AT ONCE, I TELL YOU! YOU ARE TO RUSH TO HER LADYSHIPSES AID! GET UP, MY BOY!"

I opened the door, and there stood Auntie Akifa in her fluffy nightgown in a sinful shade of pink, dozy Apple under one arm, the other proffering a tangle of rusty keys. I knew what they entailed.

"Oh no, no, I absolutely refuse..." I began, as the patented Auntie Akifa glare began to turn up the temperature. "I mean, the idea of sitting on a train in a mask for four hours or more was bad enough, but..."

"The train takes far too long, Banjo," Auntie Faiza bellowed in my ear, "And we wouldn't want to endanger you in an enclosed place like a train carriage, because we love you."

"Oh, well thank you so very much for that," I fumed. "But there is no way that... Not TREVOR."

"TAKE THE KEYS, BANJO WAKO!"

I grimaced, and accepted the tangle of old leather and metal. The keys to Trevor, a rusted 125CC Lambretta which young Faiza loudly (of course) roared around on in her uni days, but which now haunted the cluttered garage beneath our flats. I hadn't so much as touched it for nobody knows how many yonks, but although I've never had a full license, I did somehow pass my scooter tests to bumble around West London on him in my noughties days.

"Auntie Faiza, I haven't parked my bum on this rusted old heap of junk since Britney was in the charts!"

"Don't bad-mouth Trevor, my boy, he'll get you there!" the reply boomed over speaker-phone. "I forgot to say, I did find a very skilled professional to give him a quick MOT and a bit of a tune-up. You were out shopping, but Akifa let her in."

There lurched Trevor, looking perhaps a little more shiny than I would have given him credit for after all this time, and affixed to the fuel tank was one of those old scientific plastic labels, with 'TREVOR EXPERIMENT IV' punched into it. I was impressed to note that a brand new winking phone charger had been subtly attached to the steering column, and on the seat perched a steel water bottle, with another punched label: "DRINK ME".

'Most amusing', JJ must have thought. Of course, she couldn't just be a chemical master, she had to have supernatural engineering powers too.

"Oh, I simply can't thank you enough!" I sarcastically bellowed. "Certainly, not with any real sincerity."

But both aunties ignored me. "JJ said to say," Auntie Faiza yelped in my earhole, "dear old Trevor was as souped-up as a brand new model, with a full tank, just rev him up and head east." My dear trouble-making flesh and blood let out a roaring lion's yawn. "We're all counting on you, babs. Night night, Banjo."

"But wait a minute, aged relative, I mean, for fff–" I tried to protest, but the line was dead.

"Packed you some sandwiches," Auntie Akifa said, as if accusing me of forcing her to wipe my bumhole, "Now, Benjamin, put on some sensible apparel, and then you can bally well go and you prove yourself, at last."

I wanted to say "I am already pretty incontrovertible proof of myself", but I slunk upstairs and obeyed, donning my bespoke long hooded raincoat, and was soon facing an open garage door and planting my pristine Allbirds on Trevor's footplate. There wasn't a fleck of dawn to be seen beyond the garage, but I accepted the sandwiches, and was terrified for a moment that Auntie Akifa was going to kiss me good bye. But she limited herself to a pat on the shoulder, stifled a yawn, and slurred "I'm going back to bed now." A pause. "You're a good one, Banjo."

Stunned at what amounted to a tsunami of auntie devotion, coming from her, I plugged my phone into the charging bank, screwed in my earphones, clicked on the map link sent to me by Auntie Faiza, and gazed at the blue line headed to the metropolis. I slid my Sungod Vulcans onto my nose and opened the bottle of what I presumed was Buck-Up reserve. With a single gulp, the stars seemed to lurch like a *Star Trek* warp, and I started Trevor up. And, I began following that blue line.

Perhaps it was the effect of JJ's elixir, but what I feared would be a neighbourhood-waking snarl-and-putter from Trevor seemed to me more of a purr than ever it had been. It was 3:53 a.m. Five hours to complete 160 miles. There were better times to tell yourself "Let's do this", but I did.

Nobody trundles from Shropshire down to South London in the middle of the night with a light heart. It was cold, it was boring, it was greatly painful in the glutes division. Only the odd sip of Buck-Up kept me going. I can pretty much measure that ridiculous voyage in albums listened to on the road down to Hereford, Worcester, and whatnot – three of mine, one by The Who, plus a Beyoncé best of. Though I expected to have to refuel somewhere around Oxfordshire, to my recurring amazement, Trevor's fuel gauge was still only quietly slipping down from Full as I slowly purred and puttered my way Reading-wards, a suitably pink and gob-smacking dawn creeping over the heavens as I passed the Big City on the left hand side.

I swung Trevor past the seemingly endless railings of Dulwich College, in search of some auction house called 'PUP Art Inc', which turned out to be squatting on the corner of a leafy back street in south-east London, at Valley Fields. Pretty place.

The journey had squashed and squished my lissom frame about as much as a voyage through a black hole would. I dismounted, stretched, and perched on a nearby garden wall. There were a few sploshes of Buck-Up reserve still in the bottle, and I decided it would be wise to unscrew it and have another gulp for the ordeal ahead. The sun was warm on the ivy-covered garden wall, bees were tootling as they tucked in to a boss buffet of blooms, and the birds seemed to be singing a lullaby...

That must have been my very last thought before I was suddenly shaken awoke in the all-too-warm morning sunshine, because the next thing I knew an affronted homeowner was out in his garden jostling me from behind with a broom, grumping, "Hoi, you can't just kip on my garden wall y'know, mate, buzz away off with you!" A glance at my phone informed me that it was 9:19 a.m. and time for me to let out a loud "YARGH-OOOH!" The Valley-Fielder's broom had somehow become entangled with the hood of my coat, and I was tugged back sharply over a far steeper garden wall than I had imagined, landing thankfully on something soft – but unthankfully, it was a mucky and steaming pile of something which only roses could find delicious.

The old gentleman with a broom looked instantly apologetic, and was stammering all sorts of intentions of brushing me down and whatnot, but

I had no time to offer anything but a "Sorry, cheers mate!" before I scrambled back up onto the pavement, and hared down the road on foot.

I skidded around the corner, pelted into the gilt doors of PUP Art, Inc, then through them, clattered up the reception steps, and crashed into the first double-doors which came my way, from where a droning voice was heard describing some item of art which he didn't seem to want to glance at for more than half a second.

"... Early twentieth century, which we know thanks to the dating on the painting, of 1923. Still familiar to some as the basis of the popular advertising campaign for a now defunct brand of soup–"

"UUUUUM, HEY! NOW STOP THE AUCTION NOW PLEASE!" I yelled — and muffled screams rang out.

I had barged right onto the auctioneer's podium, in front of about forty mask-wearing art-lovers. Perhaps my sudden appearance, bedraggled, with mask and shades on, clutching a metal bottle, might have seemed somewhere in the region of a bit freaky on a Monday morning, but I still don't believe it deserved the rugby tackle I received from a gigantic brother in a dark blue jumper, who pinned me to the ground and gazed up at the master of ceremonies for some kind of further order.

A dizzying flurry of mask-muffled outcries filled the hall:

"Is that a bomb?"

"Someone send for Little Mr. Purvis!"

"What is that *ferocious* hummage?!"

"Have the toilets bust again?"

"What's that tit up to there?"

"Get *off* him, Gary!"

"Are we bidding yet?"

"It's an ugly picture anyway."

"Ah, germ warfare, is it?"

"Is it the PC brigade at last?"

"Somebody's spilled my Bovril!"

"Well, I'M not taking the knee for anybody!"

"Little Mr. Purvis has been sent for!"

As my struggle continued, presently a grinding whine began to quieten the flustered crowd, as a leather stairlift creaked down the stairs beyond the open door, and perched on it was a dusty vision in tweed jacket and Bermuda shorts. In time, two socked-and-sandalled feet hobbled onto the stage beside me, above them the whitest hairless legs I had ever seen, and somewhere beyond, a slack-jawed old birdy man, clearly the boss everyone was suddenly grovelling to.

"Mr. Purvis, sir, we had barely begun today's proceedings when this, this youth bursts through the door and..."

"Mr. Purvis, he's got a bomb!"

"One of these All Black Lives Matter bunch, I'll be bound, Little Mr. P!"

"Will everyone shut up, please?" the ancient arrival croaked, with a weak cough from beneath his face mask. "Gary, get off him."

"Little Mr. Purvis, Sir!"

Suddenly free from Gary's tungsten grip, I staggered to my feet, and tried to chill things out as best I could.

"I'm sorry about this, but it's not a bomb, it's a bottle."

"He says it's not a bomb, it's a bottle," Little Mr. Purvis repeated, taking hold of my metal bot of B.U. Special Brew with the confidence of a bloke who surely was down to his last few Christmases. "It's always the same. Why must there always be such a hullabaloo every time I take my early morning nap, Spencer, will you tell me that? I happen to be feeling particularly death's door-y today as it happens, so if you can't be trusted to oversee a simple auction of assorted tat, then–" Old Little Mr. Purvis began to break down into extended coughs, which caused a tremor of terror among the carefully socially-distanced mob, despite the boss wearing a mask in a fetching shade of puce. It seemed only kind to intervene.

"Blimey, look, I've not got any virus, I've given the top a wipe, please do take a sip, it's just a Buck-Up energy drink," I offered, not least as the absent-minded Little Mr. Purvis had already screwed the top off my bottle and was sniffing the contents. With a gargle which I think passed for thanks, he pulled his mask to one side, lifted the metal canister to his spluttering lips and took a hefty gulp.

"Gah!" He gasped. "I've not touched this stuff for years, but it's still like drinking sherry from a sweaty shoe." He gave one final lung-clearing cough, and turned to me with a new sparkle in his watery eyes. "Ah, you must be the explanation for that eccentric text message I awoke to last night. You're here for the Yaxley jumble?"

I nodded my assent, the room somehow stepped off terrorist alert, and everyone returned to their seats, to fan themselves with auction leaflets and tut to each other about the delay to their lots coming up.

"Good-oh! So what were you doing sprawled on the floor with our security staff all over you? Very odd behaviour."

The auctioneer butted in. "Mr Purvis, this gentleman stormed his way into the room, and I believe it was the correct procedure to..."

"Correct procedure in a lamb's fat arse, Spencer!" Little Mr. Purvis boomed with a new-found strength. "I thought I had made myself clear before the end of business on Friday, that these Yaxley lots were not to be included in today's sale! Do I have to do everything around here? Well, young man, you come on up to my office immediately, and you can bring that hideous dawb with you. Pip pip!" And to the astonishment of his underlings, their mummified head manager whispered a few words to the master of ceremonies, then pulled on his toes, and hopped up the grand wooden staircase like a lad a fifth of his age.

The thoroughly disgusted auctioneer approached me with a large tin of Haze, and sprayed me in every direction, before picking up a huge canvas, and pushing it into my outstretched arms without a word of apology – except to the amassed bidders and sellers, to whom he then crooned, "Apologies for the delay, everyone, lots 214 through to 229 are no longer in today's auction, so we move along to lot 230..."

I staggered out of the auction hall, and was a bit phased to find myself eyeball to eyeball with that cue-ball-throated chinless father of Ladies Angela and Bobbie, the long-gone Earl of Yaxley, looking forever like a lobotomised kid in a candy shop. As I loped up the stairs, his hungry look almost seemed to be grateful to me, having valiantly saved him from being flogged off by a repellent distant descendent.

Little Mr. Purvis was not approving. "A very early Pendlebury, 1923, I believe, personally I'd say it's worth roughly the price of fire wood, if it were not for the, I believe they now style it, 'Retro' nature of the advertising history of the thing. I remember those Slingsby's Soups, they used to have those TV adverts, *'Soups dooo something to me...'* " the old man sang with a surprisingly strong falsetto, but those were clearly the only words which had wedged themselves into his old grey cells, and so he changed the subject. "... Something like that anyway. What on earth made you so awfully desperate to retrieve it?"

"Mr. Purvis, I've been travelling all the way from Shropshire since three in the morning to stop the sale of this painting."

"Have you never heard of email, young man?" he chortled. "Halfway across the country, *'I drove all ni-ight, to get to you...'* all for an obscure portrait like this!"

His repeated swerves into pop lyrics were beginning to make me enjoy the company of this Little Mr. Purvis, but I was starting to twig that some great gag had been pulled at my expense, as if Ant and Dec were about to spring out at me and admit that by now they really were desperate for J-list celebrities to prank.

"I was told that the Yaxley auction could only be stopped in person!"

"How very queer. You're friends with Heather, aren't you? We used to knock about a bit back in the swinging days. It's not like Heather to fail to grasp something so basic, I thought I had explained the situation fully to her over the phone, the junk was safe, and so was her father's letter. Admittedly, that knob-end Spencer nearly flogged it all off after all, most regrettable, I'd sack him if I could. But well done, nonetheless, that's quite some mission of mercy you've completed. Something to tell the grandkids, what?"

"I don't even want the painting, it looks like a cross between Plug and Lord Snooty. But I was told that the daughters of this weirdo were desperate to get it back after Troy Van Hurl had begun to clean out their family treasures."

"And you wanted to help them?"

"Well... yeah. I suppose, yes I did."

"Say no more, Mr...?"

"Wako. Banjo Wako."

"Say no more, my dear Banjo. You wanted to spread some happiness. And you have achieved it. You know, there's far too much blether about capitalism these days, if you ask me, I've given a long and not uncomplicated life to Art, and I never saw any reason for doing so, other than to be happy, and make others happy. My dear old father, Peter Purvis the first, Lord rest his sweet soul, first established Purvis Ukridge Psmith Art Incorporated – P.U.P. you understand, because the P was silent..."

I nodded as if he was making any sense at all.

"...As in triceratops."

I nodded harder.

"The three of them hooked up at one of the clubs and agreed to start the company nearly halfway through the last century, buying up much of the defunct Spencer Gregson gallery, and all members of the original triumvirate were confident the business would thrive. Papa's co-investors, messrs Psmith and Ukridge, nice enough chaps both, may have had their own reasons for getting into the art racket – money, I recall, had its part to play for at least one of them. But my Papa, you know, he was different, he was young, he was idealistic, and Art with a capital A meant more to him."

The sweet old geezer was clearly just settling merrily into his soliloquy, and as the rigours of my long evening had left me in a more powerless fug than usual, and he seemed keen to tell me all about his old man, I was happy to listen. Having never had an old man of my own, tales of fatherly advice often drew my attention.

"Sounds like a nice bloke!" I said.

"Oh, he really was, bless him. You'd have loved him. Small story for you. He always used to proudly share this memory of one time when he was just a young lad at school, and on one memorable School Prizes day there was some very clever fellow – one of these stern men of business they

186

used to get to hand out the school prizes in those days – and my father got some book or something as a prize, and as he went to pick it up, right there on the stage, this chap looked right into Papa's eyes and said to him the words, 'It's a beautiful world, full of happiness on every side'. He never forgot the words, and nor shall I. That somewhat became my father's motto in life, and Sir Peter Kevin Purvis always insisted that the Beauty of Art heaped beauty on the beautiful. That's what we're here for. This bloody awful Pendlebury scribble here may qualify for these fine sentiments, I think it also may not, but the pursuit of happiness remains paramount, I hope. So please, my dear Mr. Wako, do take this terrible portrait, and its contents, with the warmest compliments of PUP Art Inc."

I thanked him uncertainly, and began the clearly nightmarish task of wrestling the huge canvas back out into the suburban sunshine. There was also a cardboard box containing other bits and bobs – a posh ashtray, a bent golf club, a sickening little blob I was informed was an Infant Samuel at Prayer. What the frick Van Hurl thought he was doing offering these knick-knacks to this obscure *Flog It* emporium was beyond me, but then so much seemed to be by this stage.

"Buck-Up Special Brew, you say?" the old fellow laughed as we shook hands, "I must see if I can get a few bottles of that for myself."

It was only when I was back down on the street with Trevor and the enormous Lord Yaxley that I realised there was no plan beyond this point, and all for nothing, I had been dumped in South London with the supposed order to try and transport a gigantic framed painting 160 miles north-west on the back of a Lambretta. Words were spoken. Loud, spiky ones. Until, that is, the weeding inhabitants of Valley Fields began to raise eyebrows at the noise, and I decided to seethe for a while instead.

There was no way I was going to try to get that ugly painting home the same way I had come, and it was just as I was beginning to compose a particularly withering text to my Auntie Faiza to that effect, when I remembered that the name 'Valley Fields' should have been ringing a few bells for me – albeit little bells at first, on far away hills.

Of course, this was where the Mels had set up home! Throughout all the noughties tours endured by The Fresh Drones, my survival had been all-but the responsibility of the great Mel Medlicott, *the* roadie's roadie in the pop tour universe. Six foot three if she was a millimetre – which she wasn't – with cascades of ginger curls, muscles upon rippling muscles, and a laugh like a reversing pantechnicon, lovely old Mel may actually have been the closest thing I had to the old aforementioned G.A. back in the Fresh Drones days, the mensch of mensches. I had played at her wedding to even hairier fellow road manager legend, and walking five-piece settee, Mel Willis, roadie of choice for the squirty cream of UK pop, but had never got round to visiting them at their Valley Fields semi! They would have a shower, and coffee, and unquestionably, a massive van.

I was just about to try and dig out Mel's number when a sound emerged from a nearby One-Stop very like a reversing pantechnicon. It's a small world. Or perhaps a very large one, where coincidences regularly occur.

## Chapter Thirteen

Having been welcomed into the Mels' gloriously homey home, Mel M was just insistently pushing me into a roomy bathtub filled with pink unicorn bubbles and glitter, while Mel W shoved my stinking threads in the wash and cooked up a pan of glistening Linda McCartney burgers, when of course, the messages started to ping in:

'JOB A GOOD UN? WHERE ARE YOU, YOUNG HOUND? Fx'

The effect of the unicorn bubble bath was only just kicking in, so I chose to turn off my phone just that once, and savour the moment. Once marginally less stinky, freshly towelled off and clad in a random 'Fresh Drones 2009' tour hoody and sweatpants (or, as I prefer to think of them, perspiration trousers), I flomped – if that's the word I'm after, Spellcheck seems unconvinced – into one of the Mels' many gigantic beanbags which equated the happy couple's entire furniture range, tucked into a welcome elevenses and prepared to trounce my kindly hosts in seven degrees of Videogame Character Kart Racing. It had been at least a couple of years since last we had hung together like this, especially with all the lockdown palaver, and the day just grooved away, through to dinner, with talk of bad old days, of ridiculous riders and Japanese power cuts, before I finally dared to switch the old phone back on.

37 messages, 13 of them voice messages. I let out an exclamation which caused the Mels to cock eyebrows at each other. I showed them the screen, and dared to open one at random.

"Banjo darrrrling," Poppy purred into my ear, "Where have you got to, you naughty Elven King? Jocasta and Lemmy have just hitched up from Glastonbury, and I promised them that you would be able to put them up? You'll love them both as deeply as I do, I'm sure. In fact, they were telling me all about all these benefits you can get when you're in a marriage partnership, and... well, that's a lovely discussion for when we're finally face to face again. Face to face to creamy..."

I dropped my phone in recoil, and it automatically clicked onto what seemed to be the most recent of a few dozen voicemails from Auntie Faiza.

"WELL ALL I CAN SAY IS, YOUR DNA AIN'T GOT NOTHIN' TO DO WITH MINE, YA LIL LOUNGE GECKO! WE WAS EXPECTING YOU FOR TEA AT THE LATEST, THERE'S IMPORTANT PEOPLE HERE! ALL I CAN SAY IS–"

Mel M, the Boudicca of boombox-yompers, took the phone right out of my hand, and arose to pause the spin of *Kind of Blue* while bringing the phone to her ear.

We heard it ringing. We heard it bellowing. "BANJO, YOU BLOODY–"

"OH MY GOD IT'S REALLY FAIZA MALONE!" Mel crowed, "I'm sorry, I've worked with some of the biggest pop stars on the planet but as a girl from Kiddy, let me just say this is a real honour..." was all we heard, before she strode out into the tiny garden, closing the patio door as she went.

With those two blaring away, of course Mel W and I could make out all sorts of gysts as to what was being said, with audio highs from my ex-roadie including "I GUARANTEE YOU" and "HE BLOODY DONE IT! HE

ONLY BLOODY DONE IT!" and "THAT MAN IS A STAR!" and those from the other end of the line discernible as "ALWAYS, HE LANDS ON HIS FEET!" and "YOU JUST GOTTA GET HERE!"

Eventually, Mel M returned, and handed me back the phone.

"All settled. We're leaving first thing in the morning – well, we've all had too many turbo shandies to crawl up to the West Midlands now – but we can get all your bric-a-brac and Trevor in the back of the van. Lovely lady, you never told me Faiza Malone was your Auntie, Banjo!"

"Never heard of her," Mel W protested.

"Ah, but you're from Cornwall, y'dolt, they had different news people down there."

"Ar."


It was a surprisingly fresh and colourful Tuesday morning when we old Millennials had our road trip back across the belly of Britain – I recommend the egg muffins at the Cricklade Welcome Rest. We were just returning smug old Trevor to store, and I was showing off my crib to both Mels, when we saw the post it notes all over the door – "CASTLE! NOW!" being the theme of most of them. One simply screamed in red, 'MY LORD!'

Well, it seemed rude not to, and the Mels volunteered that they regularly paid over the odds to visit places as National Trusty as Yaxley Castle, so up we chugged, and I was soon lugging the painting out of the back of the van.

"Yes yes yes," I grumbled as I struggled with the frame, "The mother-LOVIN' conquering hero is home, replete with hideous cartoon of plug-ugly toff, one, rescued from London auctioneers, yes-ter-day..." My partially rehearsed opening volleys on seeing Auntie Faiza at the grand doorway of the Castle tailed off as I saw the look on her face. It was emblazoned with her usual Cheshire-cat-who-got-the-cream-thanks-to-her-own-curiosity broad grin, but I knew her eyes well enough to see something else, a look of pity I suppose, which brought me up short. It reminded me of that time, as a twelve-year-old, when I had assured her that I was going to be bigger than Little Richard, just before I fell off the family piano straight into our late pussy Muggeridge's quite voluble and toxic litter tray.

"Banjo," she smiled, as if she was interviewing me for a *Midlands This Evening* section on – what? art salvagers? "It's lovely to see you at last. It's best that you come straight on in, everyone's waiting in the Grand Hall."

"I pardon yours, Auntie? Who? Everyone's what?" I said, following her with concern. Presumably the Mels were as wide-eyed as anyone who first entered those portals and gazed up at the armour, flag, lethal weapon, golf club and extinct animal head-festooned rafters of Yaxley Castle. I was pretty over it by now, but I was more concerned with the vision which lay before me – all five 'aunts' at once.

Faiza and Akifa, in her Sunday best, to the west, to the east, the Ladies Angela and Bobbie. JJ hovered respectfully at a distance.

From the west:

"How dashed NICE of you to join us at last, young Benjamin!"

From the east:

"Oh GOD'S FAT NADS at LAST! Old blue eyes is back!"

"Ah, and with Daddy's portrait too, too kind!"

"Banjo, darling, I have a shoal of ravenous garra rufa in Bewdley who are supposed to be nibbling all the nasty bits off my little tootsies by 4.30, and the little loves do get so hungry without my visits. Let's get on, shall we? Loves?"

And centre, my benevolent employer, Mrs. J. She had nothing to give me but a truly blazing smile which I'd never seen her attempt before. She had clearly just been in conversation with some other dude, entirely new to me.

Unlike most of the room's occupants, he was of a similar vintage to myself, perhaps a few years older, though with dress sense and mannerisms more on the Sanatagen-side, with sandy hair and tidy beard, and glasses on a gold chain. He strode along the carpet and, with no question of touching elbows, gave me a firm handshake. "Banjo Wako, I say. A great, great pleasure, got to say, have to say, and said. My name is Armine Herring," he said, with the air of a man who could never quite get used to the fact. "I have been the Mannering-Phipps' legal advisor and representative for nearly twenty years, since my father shuffled off the old mortal perch. And I have never known a year like this, sir, let me say! Loved – what was it? 'Happy Joy Sunny Song', or whatever it was?"

"*Summer Yet Again!*"

"That's the pine marten. Look, perhaps you should have a bit of an old sit down, dear chap, long journey and all that, are there any refreshments?"

JJ approached with a salver of what presumably was more than impeccable alcohol of some kind. It turned out to be a properly crusty brandy. Could have done with some diet cola of some kind, but it took the edge off the nerve-

jangling of this unexpected welcome.

"Iiiiit's toffee-sticky tricky to be sure where to start with this old thing, yes?" The lawyer continued once we had all bent the knees. "Hang on, oh gosh of course, I forgot the most important thing."

Herring crossed to the corner of the vast Hall, where Mrs. J and a hitherto shadow-hugging JJ were busy examining and turning over the huge canvas which had long been loosened from my grip. The trio conferred in whispers, and examined a sheaf of stapled paper which seemed to have been magicked up. In little time, he returned and sat down.

"Yes, it's all there. Banjo, you are the rightful 18th Earl – well, you should have been the 17th Earl, but for goodness sake let's not lower the tone – you are, as I say, gosh yes, surely – no, legally, it's true, you are – it's official – the rightful 18th Earl of Yaxley."

There was something of a pause. A beat, then more beats.

"...Lovely to meet you!" he beamed. "As I say."

The story unfolded so laughably fluidly, like treacle down a weirdo's naked back. In the years before my melodramatic toilet debut, The Hon. Reginald Mannering-Phipps had been drafted in to use his preternatural powers of gig-fixing capability to aid the charitable dreams of a rag-taggle bunch of pop stars, as a brand new civil war began to rage in the Sudan. He quickly established a commanding knowledge of how to play the country's ragged system like a flute, to ensure aid got to where it needed to be, and on a follow-up jaunt as part of a Comic Relief scouting party, he had met and fallen sandals over quiff in love with Laila Amina Wako, the beaming receptionist at the Juba city council, or whatever the official base was called. She was twenty-three, and the blue-eyed posh boy a well-maintained forty-six. I've always been a bit of a dong at the Maths, but even I knew enough to raise my eyebrows and waggle them.

All there professed absolute ignorance of all this ancient history – Lady Angela and Bobbie were bringing up their own children at the time, and Faiza was still young. Mrs. J seemed tempted to interject – her upper lip quivered for the slightest fraction of a second – but remained silent as the pieces were fitted together.

"Christ on a crap segway, Banjo!" Mel M gasped. "Our next door neighbour Terrence is 72. Born in the West Indies, came here at six months, worked in the Dulwich library since The Beatles was still going. Last week, they called Terrence up for repatriation to a place he only visited once on holiday – but you! You only turn out to be the Lord of to the fuh-flip-frickin'... manor born!"

"Ere, love – this looks like a family do to me," Mel W looked uncomfortable. "Let's get, eh?"

Mel M had to agree. "Would anyone be too arsed – I mean, would you mind – if we did have a bit of a look round though? We love all this."

"Of course," Lady Bobbie waved her assent, to Angela's disapproval. "I recommend the Red Room – apparently Ivor Novello used to nut in there at parties!"

"It's all been thoroughly cleaned, I assure you." Lady Angela sniffed, and my travel buddies legged it.

Auntie Akifa seemed frozen, but Auntie Faiza touched me on the knee like I was a hospice inmate in one of her Special Reports. "Banjo, my boy, let me tell you, all this was news to me, which kills me, because news is what I do. I was just a kid, our Daddy had been killed, and we had to get out of Juba, that was all I understood."

Back in the eighties, through the Hon's exertions, a place was found in a West Midlands boarding school for Faiza, and with my grandfather, poor Ayman Wako, being toast, and my cells dividing like Grease Lightning, it only left for Reggie to do – of course – The Honourable Things, wed Laila and get back home to Blighty, with all Laila's loved ones.

"All Laila told me in her last letter was that I had won a scholarship! I thought that made me so clever too..."

"But you were!" her sister blurted out.

"You are." Mrs. J added.

"They must have talked to you about it, Akifa?" Faiza boomed at her older sister, who sat there still with the unaccustomed look of a hunted boar who had better things to do.

"I remember nothing. I choose to remember nothing. Nothing happened. Dash it all!" Auntie Akifa was insistent – until her glance met Mrs. J's and stiffened automatically into the trademark Auntie Akifa glare. But this time, Mrs. J glared back, in an ocular play on the clash between red and blue lightsabers, and that famous glare puttered out. With difficulty, my auntie finally began to open up in a manner utterly new to me, after a lifetime of smarting at her protective prickles. "Juba was my home. I knew that Laila was in love with some man, some impossible man from the books she read, it seemed to me. I had no time for that 'Comic Relief' rot. I had my own life, I was young, I had the church. I loved Laila. We both loved Laila. But she never told me nothing, no matter how I tried to prise it out of her, except that she was in love. And then her belly began to grow, in the name of the Good Lord, and then of course, ho ho!" – never had the two words conveyed less mirth – "this magic man was long gone, wasn't he?"

The *Who Do You Think You Are* narrative deepened, as there was no clue as to why Reggie, the Honourable, had been forced to leave his heavily pregnant partner on her own, chartering a jet co-owned by Izzy McIzmo, but he seems to have made a final visit home to Dinham only weeks before I was born, to everyone's amazement.

"We hadn't seen him since the spring, had we, Roberta?" Lady Angela offered.

"The last time I saw our big brother," Lady Bobbie's voice broke a little, "He was dancing at my wedding. Doing the Funky Chicken, I remember clearly. My first wedding. No, second."

When it seemed to be Mrs. J's turn to throw something into the ring, she simply said, "Do read it out, Mr. Herring."

He held a note, taken from the envelope which had been hidden behind the portrait.

"'6th June 1987. Dear Mr. J'," he began, "'I know you will forgive me both for the brevity of the note, and for the danger of entrusting it to poor old Bill to pass on to you. The truth is, sir, I'm in love like you would not believe. I had hoped to catch you on this flying visit and tell all, I know if you could meet Laila you would approve, and understand, as you always do. But Papa and especially Mama will be more than a little difficult, after all these years of bachelorhood, especially when they learn that we are already married. And have a little one not far from popping out. Yes, I know, I should have told you about this before, and I am awfully sorry. Our wedding was a hasty affair in a bullet-riddled Baptist chapel in Juba, but yes, I have officially jumped off the dock, and I have never been so happy, sir. That is why I know you would approve, and I feel sure dear old father would too. After you had done a little patient explaining to the old boy. How Mater will react I cannot predict. Probably set off fireworks in our faces or something. But you could  win even her around, I'm sure. I was hoping that, if armed with the evidence, you might be able to cook up some kind of warming pan to the whole idea of the next of the Mannering-Phippses being half Sudanese? I enclose the wedding certificate, and we will be flying home together at the end of the month. I know you will be able to offer your usual sage ripostes to their inevitable expostulations one way or another. Pip pip and warm wishes for now, your friend, Reggie. P.S. Against better judgement, I have had to entrust this letter to poor Billy, stressing to him its utmost import, and that under no circumstances must Mummy see it before it reaches your hands. Surely even he would be able to get this to you without messing things up.' ...Clearly not', Herring concluded. Lady Bobbie groaned:

"Just like Billy to hide it in the nearest place, and forget he ever had it."

"Silly Billy", her sister sadly agreed.

"There is also a photograph," Herring gently added, and passed it on to me. A faded polaroid showed me a tall lissom blue-eyed toff in short sleeves and waistcoat, arm in arm with my mother, Laila Wako, clad in the simplest white frock, which failed to hide a sizeable bump – me. Both were wearing grins as wide as the whole of Sudan.

Of all the trickling tears before me, it was Mrs. J's which took me most by surprise. Like a vase of elegant dried flowers suddenly producing a bunch of grapes. Although she had not been able to prevent a large wet tear overflowing from her usually sandbagged ducts, however, her voice was as level and business-like as usual as she asked the lawyer for confirmation:

"Mr. Herring, we are now fully equipped to complete the legal procedures to secure His Lordship's formal investiture?"

"Yes, well ordinarily in such a circumstance, the most obvious potential source of legal complication would be the co-partners in Yaxley Ales and associated industries, but in this circumstance..."

Mrs. J's left cheek dimpled in a near-smile. "We don't foresee any objections," she said.

Herring let his glasses dangle to crotch height, and he scratched his head. "I must admit I don't much fancy taking on the might of the Van Hurl family's New York lawyers, truth be told. But thankfully I was able to grab a few words with Van Hurl's son via Zoom, and from what he says, the family is more than happy to have nothing to do with Yaxley Castle – it seems their stocks have been plummeting in the US ever since their CEO first started... and I think I'm quoting Mr Van Hurl Junior correctly here..." He pierced the air with finger quotes. "'screwing around like he was some kinda Medieval Duke of Brexitland'..."

"Sounds like you've swerved a regular visit from your American cousins, Banjo!" Auntie Faiza crowed.

"Apparently it didn't play well with the American shareholders either," Herring proceeded, "One of his son's loose-lipped representatives on social media has been vociferously distancing the company from the English aristocracy, apparently it played very badly with them over there. Presumably this news will be a relief to them, and in fact we may have been on safe grounds just with the DNA results, even without this new evidence."

"DNA results?" I gaped, and my eyes rested on JJ. Her eyes zoomed from mine to fix on some glinting piece of warmongering scrap which was affixed high on the ceiling, before returning, with palpable apology, to mine.

"I deeply apologise for the necessity of the deception, Banjo – it was only a few stray hairs, from a hairnet. But being owed a number of favours by the Head Scientist of a private testing centre in Bonn, as I am, it seemed wisest to uncover the truth, to settle our own minds, at first."

"Not wanting to get the old boy's hopes up for a load of fantasy, you mean?"

She almost smiled. "Something like that. With the future of the estate in such dire projection at the time, the very real possibility of having this hypothesis disproved, and publicly, could have been..."

"A trifle embarrassing," Mrs. J concluded.

"One little bit of jigsaw blue sky I can't quite locate," Herring was literally scratching his head like a forlorn Stan Laurel, "Is how you managed to safely bring Benjamin – I mean, His Lordship..."

"Banjo is fine."

"... How you managed to make your way here, Mrs. Wako, after the sad loss of your sister?"

Herring quailed like a man who suddenly realised his briefs were soaked in lighter fuel as Auntie Akifa blazed one of her fieriest stares at him, but the look softened as she gave a voluble gulp, like Apple that time he managed to swallow an entire scotch egg, and her storytelling petals unfurled further:

"Poor Laila had been saving, waiting for this man, this Honourable man, to show up. I took the boy, once he was clean and crying well, and we managed to arrange a certificate from the doctor, the day before that surgery was bombed. Laila had been at me for so long about Great Britain – 'come home with us, Akifa, there the grass is green, and one day we can return to peace!' Always the green hills of Britain, this man had filled her up with, as well as filling her up with..." Her gaze swept onto me, and I could have shaved with it. "So I used Laila's savings to purchase two aeroplane tickets. The jessie boy on the flight desk was most impertinent, I remember. Said we had the wrong blighted papers, we couldn't fly to Britain. So I gave him a peace of my mind!"

Everybody there understood.

"... Eventually he saw sense and waved us through onto the plane without any more of his perishing red tape fussinesses. We flew here to make a home for Benjamin, and for Faiza in the holidays. I found a B&B, not without difficulty – so many white vinegar faces on the doorsteps – but from my first Sunday in the blessed church of St. Boniface's, with the dear Reverend Stinker-Byng on our side and God in our hearts, we discovered where our home is. When the flats got built, he got us straight in there, Lord bless his ghost."

Auntie Faiza looked dazed. "Some journalist I am, all this drama right under my bloody nose all my life. Though to be fair I was a bit distracted at that time by the burgeoning career of Jason Donovan. But all these years, Banjo, you've been walking these streets, propping up that bar, and all the time..."

"Astonishing how these things somehow take time to, sort of, bub, bubble up, is it not?" Herring stammered. "So, there's all sorts of paperwork to be done now we have this evidence, sir, how would you like to proceed?"

Everyone, as per usual, was looking at me. I closed my eyes, and drew a deep breath of dusty Yaxley Castle air.

"First of all, I think I would really benefit from taking myself off for a bit of a walk, a ponder, a chance to get my brain into some kind of normal gear. But actually, before that, if you're offering legal services, I need to go and get hold of the Mels, and find out the address of that Terrence Whatsisname bloke."

My dazed wander took me naturally down the hill to home, and I was just fumbling for my keys preparing to park my carcass on the sofa and mull, when I was stunned by a sudden and vociferous smack across the chops.

"LORD BANJO, I PRESUME?!" thundered Poppy Pirbright. I don't know why, but I'll admit, she was looking particularly gorgeous as she stood there in the midday sun, hair a jagged jangle of orange and puce, and face a strikingly sharp mask of simmering scorn. As ever, she seemed dressed for Day 5 of the filthiest Glasto binge, and the effect was a bit spoiled by the pile of luggage and laundry behind her, and two decidedly shifty-looking hairy kids who were new to me.

"You – how could you already...?" I began. It seemed that when deep dark secrets are kept bottled up for a few decades, popping the cork meant that suddenly truth was gushing all over the place, all over your shoes, trodden into the carpet. Subsequently, it was obvious how she knew – her rotten little father had clearly been earwigging on the whole dramatic scene, and let his daughter know in no time, perhaps with a view to begging her to trap me in a wedding ring and make herself a Countess. What a quandary for a racist snob – a Black son-in-law which finally gets your family a top-grade nob connection. But at the time, I just gibbered. "Poppy, look, I mean, I–"

"I cannot believe what I have just heard – and never you mind how I heard it – you're like the New. *Lord*? Of. *Yaxley*? Banjo Wako? And I was just, like, here, your dutiful girlfriend, suggesting to Barrabas and Angora here that we all settle in for a mind-blowing few days of growing experiences together? Suddenly I'm supposed to become, like, Lady Nazi Mitford-Whatsit of the big Castle?"

"'Snot cool, dude." One of the piles of laundry murmured.

"Yeah, I thought we was here for some of them dodgy orange sweeties!" moaned the other.

"I've cleaned that castle, Banjo, and I'm telling you, sheep wouldn't live in it. Please tell me you're going to tell them where they can stick their family inheritance? Like, like, you must realise there's simply no way I could have anything whatever to do with any cis bloke who's of the pigging Landed Gentry! Pocoyo was right, you are a..." It would be unfair of me to suggest that Poppy had the *mot juste* tattooed somewhere in the region of her armpit, but she lifted her arm violently, buried her nose in her pit, indeed sharply and began to quote, "*'You are an anachronistic parasite on the body of the state'*! You should all be hung up by the... by the..."

"Haha, Lady Poppy! Baroness Pirbright!" the slightly more bosomy of what I presume was her 'secondary couple' chuckled. "You'd just feel like spitting at your face every time you saw it in a mirror, babe."

"Shut *up*, Angora! We are done here. You see, Banjo?" Poppy suddenly smiled a dagger-slit smile, like a vet charged with putting down her own family pet, but knowing she was going to enjoy it. "There's just no way ahead for our love. Banjo. You know what? My Dad would *love* it! I'm refusing to speak to him since he provided the catering for that Van Hurl party. A friend has loaned me some money, and I'm finally going to India, with Drongo and Honoria. Well, Morocco."

"Near enough?"

"Just away, from everything. No, no, I'm sorry, sugar bear, but our days are done. I once loved you with a fire which cannot burn on a pyre built with thousands of years of rich, patriarchal, privileged rape and murder of the people to line their guts. You ARE going to tell them you'd rather die, and decline the inheritance?"

I honestly had no clue – was I? For now, I just had the usual strangulated vowel sounds which were somewhere in the region of "Well, I, um..."

"No, don't speak, Banjo. I can see you're just exactly like all the rest, with your atoms, and your... your DNA! No, you're worse. You'll let them suck you into their insane world."

"Well, I, um..."

"No, I said don't speak. Oh, Banjo. Our beauty has drifted; it's just minging. Don't text me, don't call me, I'm blocking you on every platform – don't even perv on my socials. Goodbye, my bloody LORD!"

And the three of them picked up their caravan and shuffled off towards town. Either Barrabas or Angora turned to yell at me, "Tory scum!"

The fact that this ultimate of all insults, one which had never, ever been shouted my way before and which would usually wound like the whack of a sledgehammer, utterly failed to even penetrate my mind at the time, is clear testament to the gigantic wave of relief I was surfing, as I let myself into my pad, locked the door behind me, and smiled. It felt good. After so much strife, smiling was far more 'me'.

## Chapter Fourteen

All that was a number of yonks ago, depending on your personal estimation of a yonk – but anyway, some time around the confusing conclusion of those lockdown days, and the start of what some brainstormer decided might as well be called the 'new normal'.

Not being a dude for looking back that much – a Wako family trait, clearly – I'm a bit surprised at my level of recall. I have such an astonishing short-term memory, it never ceases to surprise me. But when something this melodramatic happens to you, or around you, of course, every knob with a MacBook wants to tell your story. I said no to Netflix, BBC and ITV – at least until Auntie Faiza got round me, for her *Midlands This Evening* exclusive. I'm not being banned from eating Viv's *Salata Tomatim Bel Daqua* for anything.

But I wasn't exactly soaring over a satellite about the resultant *Midlands This Evening* special either, the edit came out far too clearly in the 'sickeningly icky' area of the spectrum, like one of those Pop Talent show sad backstories which always sent me running in the opposite direction, screaming and puking. And so, the suggestion came from my friend JJ that perhaps I should be the one to try and get my own version of events down for future bemusement once and for all. My actually-scrupulously-maintained-clothes-to-riches story.

There's an old folk superstition which says that it's really very lucky to have a lot of money, and perhaps they're right. Sometimes, it seems the things you want can't be found, not for love nor money – particularly if it's love and money you're after. But as I launched myself back into jangling-nerves-free bachelorhood, I began to feel that maybe, something good could come of this unexpected twist in my fortunes, even if it did occasionally involve putting on a silly furry robe and being dragged over to Westminster to pull off a few daft genuflecting dance moves in the direction of institutions which many of my best friends suggest would be better off with a bomb or two under them. I can rock ermine when I have to.

It was Sir Izzy McIzmo who put me onto it, now we've become neighbouring big nobs in the shire.

"I wish I was a bloody lord, love!" He giggled, when last I visited Blemsorth, "Bloody Lloyd-Webber, what good does that f-bleep-er do for anyone with his peerage? I think I'd look FANTASTIC in ermine, but I suppose they'd give it to Macca before I got a look-in. But you should get stuck in, Banjo, for what it's worth, you've got leverage to do something bostin', and any prod in the right direction has to be an improvement on the system we're all f-bleep-in' stuck with, man."

His husband gently creaked in his oar, "You are at least my husband, which I suppose makes you a countess, Izzy."

"Oh yeah!" I replied. "Or should that be count?"

"I've been called worse!"

And so, plans are far afoot – first of all, the re-opening of Yaxley Castle as YAM – an 'Academy of Music', but basically a kind of talent uni for kids

208

from all imaginable backgrounds, who've got what it takes. And I won't make them blub through a tragic backstory for a chance to make their noises. We've got proper, gorgeous studios all set up ready to record, the Ballroom makes a gob-smackingly spectacular mini-arena where we can put on proper public shows, and since my story shot through the social media portals, I have a whole backlist of interested artists begging to do workshops and play at the Hall, from Sia to Sting – even Flora K has let it be known that she is warm for a residency, unless I can think of a way of putting her off.

All the Dinham Drones are on the pay-roll, of course, finally rewarded for their mad skillz – Dobbin teaches rock history, Lotto is the technical and production professor, and Neville is master of mindless noodling. His lessons seem to be the most popular.

I was in at least two minds about saying goodbye to our flats at Wickham Mansions, but there was no stopping Auntie Akifa – she was going to live in the big castle, and nothing could stop her. And so she and Apple happily reside in the special granny flat the last-Lord-but-one had installed at the rear of the castle, and I recreated my perfect crib up in the East Wing. Everything else is all for education and larks.

None of this would have been possible without the charitable spurts of cash from Yaxley Ales, of course – though their sponsorship of YAM has also seen sales go through the roof – and then there's also the loving support of my new family, on the Mannering-Phipps side.

"Wako-Mannering-Phipps?" Aunt Angela positively shivered at her own suggestion, when I popped down to visit at the sisters' Lodge – a centuries-old pile over the way, almost half the size of Wickham Mansions on its own. "It is certainly something of a mouthful, Benjamin."

"It's a triple-barrel century, darling," Aunt Bobbie shrugged. "Can you roll me one, blessed nephew?"

Of course, some time has been spent finally hammering out a legally binding reboot of the Yaxley inheritance rules, only a few centuries late, scratching out all that old toss about only males inheriting, and I went so far as to suggest to Aunt Angela and Bobbie that under the circumstances maybe they should be the ones to take on the mantle of Lady Earl or Countess or Dame or whatever it would make them, but they happily insisted that they were glad to foist all the weight onto my shoulders.

"We'd only scrap about it relentlessly, sweet boy," Lady Bobbie laughed, "And our girls have no desire to take all this dusty history on."

"We're just glad to have the family home back in good hands, Banjo," Lady Angela agreed. "And what's all this about you writing a book, as well? It simply must run in the family!"

"Yes, everyone used to say that Daddy had the intelligence of a prawn, but he ran quite a sideline on the quiet, as a memoirist – recollections of a long life among the English well-to-do, you know. Of course, they had to change lots of the names."

Lady Angela picked a whole chunk of solid paperback profusion off a nearby shelf, battered old orange Penguins. But there was no 'Bertram Mannering Phipps' on the spines.

"Who writes a memoir under a pseudonym?" I asked.

"Well when I say he wrote," Aunt Bobbie went on, "What he'd do is go into his little study and speak into a big old wax recording machine. I think he found it a pleasant respite from Mummy, frankly, especially after the War. He'd sit in there waxing lyrical about scrapes he'd got into, his run-ins with the British fascists, golfing anecdotes, all sorts."

Her sister went on, "He had a chum from the club, a budding writer, and I believe they agreed on a special deal quite early on – Daddy posted off the recordings, or at least one of the servants did, and this brain-box fellow could be relied on to turn it all into glittering prose and all that jazz, it was quite a nice arrangement for them both."

"Oh, that ghost writer was a sweetie, absolutely! Big bald fellow, wasn't he? Remember that time the whole family went over to Long Island to pay a visit, back in the sixties? All those yapping little pekes! Oh, good luck with the book, darling nephew!"

And of course, at last, our music nights are back on, down at the Love Lounge at The Angler's – our Ecstasy In The Evening, only with greatly improved air circulation and ventilation, and careful use of microphone spoffles, as musical condoms. But it's bliss to get it back, and I and my team are going to be stretching every tendon to ensure that next year's

Din-Dins will be absolutely the best one in all its 50-plus years. How many music schools have a rock festival on their own grounds?

Oh, and finally, my melodic constipation eventually gave way, too, and The Dinham Drones' new album, *Minnie's Revenge*, is available on the usual online portals, and on CD behind the bar at the Angler's.

It was just as I stopped by the pub to help clean up after a typically magical night of musical excess that JJ appeared in the doorway with a look even more serious than usual on her generally quite unreadable face.

"My Lord..."

I gave her my by now overused look which she knew to mean 'don't address me as if I was a Beano character'.

"I apologise, Banjo... if I may ask, do you have a moment?"

"For you, dear JJ, I have a whole skip-full of moments of all descriptions."

"I'm glad to see you; I've heard from my brother that his contact in Juba is confident that they can assist in ensuring that the maximum percentage of all financial assistance we are instrumental in funnelling to the organisation will be strictly employed in the securing and distribution of humanitarian aid."

This took me a moment. "Lovely jam!" I finally offered. "So, no bombs and all that palaver?"

"We are assured not, Jasper is a furiously exacting judge of character."

"Thanks so much, JJ, keep up the great work," I replied, and made to sally down to the debris of the night before, when she gave a small cough.

"You want to watch that cough", I said.

"It's just that... my grandfather says he would be very grateful to have a few words with you, at your leisure."

Her grandfather?! The old landlord, he of the dark suit and shining forehead who could be seen not smiling in a dozen black and white photos of memorable nights of Angler's Rest yore, dotted around the snug? It had never crossed my admittedly dandelion mind that He could possibly still be around after all these years. I had to stop myself from asking whether JJ was inviting me to a séance, or to converse with an urn, two scenarios which didn't seem at all in character for a scientist of JJ's astounding brain. My puzzlement must have splashed itself clearly all over my features, as she added, "Yes, he is of an unusually advanced age, Banjo, but I guarantee you that he is far more than fully *compos mentis*. You need show no concern, grandfather simply wishes to congratulate you on your inheritance."

Well, it seemed outrageously rude not to, and so I followed her up the stairs to areas of my dear old local which I had never dared nose into in all my years propping up the bar. On the third floor, Mrs. J stood awaiting us, in the doorway to a beautiful oak-bedecked study.

"Jemima, may I?" she apologised, and motioned me to enter.

"Of course," JJ said, "I'll proceed ahead and inform grandfather of his visit." And she was gone.

"If you will forgive the liberty, Banjo–" even Mrs. J had taken to saying my name as if it was a clear second to 'My Lord', but I hoped these tics would pass with time. "This household has become something of a maelstrom of emotion of late, and it has been suggested, as a psychological necessity, to confront any and all hitherto concealed circumstances and sentiments..."

I could see that I wasn't going to escape the building without a further assault course of millions of syllables, when my dear old landlady fixed me with a soulful gaze, and changed tack:

"I loved your father, Banjo. He was the brother I never had, and the lover, that... I did." There was a totally unfamiliar blush on her marble cheekbones. "I waited for him, through all his rock and roll exploits around the world, but after the eighth proposal of marriage from my first husband, I had to examine the hypothesis that my personal goals would be far more achievable with a dependable, intelligent, financially independent man, and I said "I do". The hypothesis proved to be dramatically flawed, and I was already engaged to Jemima's father when I last saw Reggie. Or rather–" she swallowed, "I did not see him, I would not see him. His darling voice came hollering down the telephone, asking for a favour, and when I heard that he was married... I placed the receiver back in its cradle. An act of hypocrisy which has given me endless... perturbation ever since. That was the last time I spoke to The Honourable Reginald Mannering-Phipps. I have had a lifetime of people telling me that I am clever, Banjo, but how I could have looked into your eyes over this bar for the last decade or more and not made these simple connections, is the only cause of shame of comparable magnitude."

"Oh..." was the best I could give, "Think less than nothing of it, Mrs. J. Yesterday's tissues and all that."

She smiled. Yes, I caught her mouth at it again – a perceptible upturn on the left hand side. "If only your grandfather..." she began. "But no. I will let Father give his own précis of events. Do come with me, dear."

To my surprise, what I presumed to be a stationery cupboard or something opened up onto a tiny lift, not much bigger than one of those restaurant-pulley jobbies, just big enough, I suppose, for a wheelchair to fit in, but something of a crush for two. Mrs. J and I breathed in and squeezed in, and after a minute or two's juddering raises, another door opened, and we stepped out into a glorious round room, the top of the whole house, like a crow's nest where everywhere which wasn't window, gazing out over Dinham and beyond, seemed to be composed of books. Some kind of cabin of frosted glass in one corner suggested a nifty en-suite, and a large green leather armchair dominated the opposite side of the circle, with a cocktail cabinet of shining silver alongside it. In the centre of the room was a large round white bed, and over most of the bed's diameter loomed the mechanism of a gold-wrought bed table, bearing a silver salver of piping hot tea in a tiny tea service of some kind of exotic antiquity, further stacks of books, and behind it all, a whole bank of computer screens and tablets and suchlike glowing away.

In the glow of the screens, in the centre of the bed, sat – how can I put this? – a golden Buddha. It would be madness to try and summarise this old dude any other way, I've set the scene for you. Though not as rotund as your usual smiling baldie Buddha figure, this ancient gent's wide serene face bore a similar gnomic smile, like the faintest new moon. His dome-like head was completely hairless, and his skin looked like carefully crimped gold-leaf, shining in the monitor light. He was clad in the crispest pyjamas of a light grey pinstripe, and as I inched further into the room, I saw it was unfair to just say he 'sat' – he seemed to almost hover in meditation, stiff-backed and somehow beatific.

"Um, hello there," I began, but knew I had nowhere to go after that besides asking after joint pains. He raised a golden hand to his lips, and gently cleared his throat – think of an aged camel coughing his approval of a particular date.

His voice, when it came, was as papery as his skin, as if a first edition of Shakespeare's Complete Works had somehow plucked up the guts to have its say.

"My Lord, I must apologise that I am not able to stand in your presence with any degree of ease today. The passing of the years..."

"Sit, sit, sit, sit, sit, my dear, old... er... landlord. You know I have been a regular, nope, a resident minstrel, at your fine pub for donkey's yonks now?"

"I have long... admired the music you and your Drones make every Thursday night, my Lord, yes. Your Ecstasy In the Evening. From this room one can glean so much of what goes on around you, but not, I fear, always sufficient data. However, I can go further, sir, I clearly remember first ushering you around the Castle on an open day over twenty five years

216

ago, when your grandfather was still alive. Presumably you would be interested to hear something of your grandfather?"

"Ah yes, JJ mentioned something about you and him being some kind of personal gentlemen together back in the day."

"I had the honour of serving his Lordship for many extremely gratifying years, in our bachelor days, between the wars..."

"Between the wars? Baba O'Reilly, that means you must be frickin' well... Shit, I mean, sorry, that's a bit rude, but..."

"I understand that Jemima was trusting enough to elucidate you on the nature of our necessarily clandestine experimental sideline within the company."

Mrs. J slipped in, "JJ darling, offer our guest refreshment." And with enough of an eyebrow raise to suggest that she hadn't needed prompting, JJ offered around steaming little cups of a ruby red substance, and I lifted mine to my lips, bracing as if about to dive out of a plane ten thousand feet up.

"The reserve infumation is a particularly smooth iteration, but the beneficial properties of our compound remain, if I may say so, manifest, sir."

All four of us shot back gulps of the weird tea, and I for one barked like a seal on a barbecue – JJ and Mrs. J gave small but noticeable quivers, and only the old man sipped with any sign of genuine pleasure.

"The physical sensations will soon resolve, sir, you will find the results worth the momentary discomfort."

Of course, he was right. As soon as my eyeballs were snugly back in their homes, I could feel the Buck-Up Special Brew zipping around my nervous system like a gang of Vikings on a sugar high.

"*Ffffreeeow*, yes, you're right," I gasped.

"Your grandfather was a beneficiary of earlier iterations of the compound, and experienced considerable extended health himself, but after he finally succumbed to the punishment of time... It would be fair to say that I retreated, in my own advanced age, to retire to my books, and my computers, and our family experiment. If I may say so, sir, had I been less of a recluse in recent years, I feel a great deal of extreme unpleasantness within the Yaxley Estate may have been circumvented. If you will forgive me, sir, had I been able to look into your eyes, there would have been no requirement for uncertainty as to the nature of your parentage."

"Not this blue eyes stuff again..." I began, but followed the old man's eyeline over my shoulder, where I had failed to notice a large gold-framed portrait between the windows.

It was clearly the same geezer as the one I had salvaged from the Valley Fields auction house – but splashed out on canvas by a far better artist, and finally I saw what these folks had been going on about all this time. They were my eyes, all right, popping out of the face of a far more instantly likeable white dude than the moping chinless wonder with the monocle in the other pesky portrait. He was nattily attired and holding aloft a sophisticated beverage of some description, caught in eternal Cocktail Time salute.

"I once described your grandfather as mentally negligible, but that was quite wrong. He was simply a gentleman of leisure. One of those who toil not, neither do they spin..."

"Oh, I toil!" I assured him, "and I spin, at times."

"I do not doubt it, sir. Perhaps you take after your father more than your grandfather in that regard. Nonetheless, it remains the case that your grandfather was the best master a personal gentleman's gentleman ever had the pleasure to serve, sir. After his marriage and investiture as Lord Yaxley, shortly before the trouble in Europe escalated..."

Some folk have been rude enough to tell me that at times I 'goggle'. Presumably I was goggling at this point, as Mrs. J discretely interjected:

"The Second World War, Father."

"Indeed, that contretemps. Having spent some time in Hollywood, I found myself in need of a situation, and his Lordship kindly recommended to me the vacancy here at the Angler's Rest, after the sad demise of the previous publican, a Mr. Ernest Biggs. I was easily able to afford the house, grounds and brewery outright, thanks to a lifetime of carefully calculated financial risk and invention, assisted by a particular fascination for the turf. My former master and I, while taking charge of the local Home Guard, both belatedly settled down, and embarked on the creation of our own families. From the very first, your father was an avid pupil of my methods and modes of efficaciousness. Sadly, his younger brother tended to show the more mentally negligent side of his father's genes, and his sisters became different shades of their mother. But Reginald had this boundless energy, Banjo, he wanted to know everything. I set him on a study of the psychology of the individual, and although heir to the title, he keenly mastered all the trades of the perfect servant. I was so proud every time he returned here to the Angler's and told me of his exploits, extricating Beatles and Bowies from scandalous contretemps and positively puppeteering the burgeoning business of, as I recall he termed it, rock super-stardom. And above all, Your Lordship, he was loved by all, for his powers of friendship, and his Code. That I could not teach him. And that, if I may take the liberty of saying so, is surely in you, as well. Your DNA results were of course conclusive, but it was not until word reached me of your brave exploits, not just in the retrieval of the appalling Gwladys Pendlebury portrait..."

"I can only profess eternal regret for the lack of full disclosure over the auction, Banjo," Mrs. J added, "When Solly Purvis telephoned me to say that an envelope addressed to father had been discovered among the Yaxley lots, suddenly the perfect nature of the emergency occurred to me, and father agreed..."

"It did indeed bear all the hallmarks of a case for the last of the Mannering-Phipps," the old man continued. "An ideal opportunity for you to prove your natural chivalrous impulses, just as you had on one night in August up at the Castle..."

I had not prepared myself for a sudden flush of hot blood to the cheeks, but frankly, this all seemed a bit sick to me.

"What is this? I creased my brow. "Am I being puppeteered too, by a secret network of ancient white people? I've spent my life being judged for my outward shell, good and bad, but I'm my own man, the judgements I make are my own. And this is MY story."

A broad flap of brow on his shiny dome intimated a degree of abjection no doubt titanic, by the standards of his family. "Please allow me to offer my most profound apologies if the observation makes you feel in any way manipulated, Your Lordship, you must understand, you are, and always have been, the master of Yaxley. The last of the Mannering-Phippses. Even had the Van Hurl usurpation not necessitated any intervention, your rightful inheritance had to be claimed, sir. You are Earl of Yaxley. And I would also posit, sir, that you have a great number of friends, grateful friends, for whom you have done all that and more. You do follow that Code."

"The Code?"

"Indeed, sir."

"Of the Mannering-Phipps'?"

"Assuredly, sir. '*Friendship, a dear balm. A smile among dark frowns: a beloved light: A solitude, a refuge, a delight.*'"

"Hey, I do like that. Another Shakey special?"

"No, sir, the poet Shelley."

"I'll have to look her up. I just want it fully laid down, in crystal clear mono, that although I have devoted my life to spreading sweetness and light, I'm not the kind of Earl who can be twisted around anyone's fiddly digits, you understand me?"

JJ was smirking, which became her well. "Of course not, Banjo. You're the boss."

"And we are happy to serve, sir. There is a tie that binds."

"That binds what?"

"You to us, sir. A promise made to a very good friend a great number of decades ago. And now we all know beyond peradventure that you would have been, should have been, if I may observe, To the Manor Born, your lordship, a certain natural order appears to have been restored. Had I just been here at the right time in 1987, things could always have been this way. Your grandfather was in Long Island, while to my regret, I had taken a vacation, fishing in Montego Bay for a month. Had either of us been here in Dinham to meet with your father... But here, at last, you are returned to us, in your rightful place. Where you, we, can do so much good. And besides, my lord – I cannot claim omnipotence."

As I stepped out into the Dinham twilight, having cleaned up the previous night's excesses, I gazed up at the top room of the Angler's Rest as was, and thought I saw a curtain twitch. It made me smile, to my surprise. Perhaps we create our own guardian angels. Or is that too deep? All I know is, you can never have the last laugh, so just enjoy the next one.

As I set off up the hill to my Castle, echoing in my mind were the last words the old gentleman's personal gentleman had to say to me before I bowed out with thanks for the tea.

"I have always, above all, endeavoured, sir," he said to me, "To give satisfaction."

So have I, old man. So have I.

## AFTERWORD

### *An apology from JFR Stableford*

This story was written out of a deep love, as an attempt to see if a certain form of frothy, silly light comedy from a hundred years ago, a musical without songs, might be translatable to the 2020s, and have something to say about the state of things a century on. Whether there was even a grain of success in this venture, sheepish enough as it was, I cannot say. But what I can, and must say is what *Ecstasy In The Evening* is: a stone-cold case of literary blackface. It qualifies undeniably, and I hope I fully understand just how far from okay this is. I can only honestly and sincerely accept that this is the case, and use my innate privilege to offer the weakest defence, that I fell arse-first into a literary trap of my own design, and for all the obvious imponderables, my only honourable option was to try and write my way out of the mess.

I've never been one for fan fiction, but as a reader I have at times found myself wallowing blissfully in some unauthorised non-canonical extension of somebody else's fictional universe. Not particularly the forms of fan fiction which seek to simply puppet the characters of deceased geniuses, adding new plots to familiar fictional creations (though the non-canonical biography of one particular giant of English humorous literature, written by C Northcote Parkinson in 1979, always struck me as pleasingly convincing), but those which dare to allude to – or even enter – famous literary universes, but give them a different weight, and tell their own tale within that world, a la Gregory Maguire's *Lost* with *A Christmas Carol* or Moore & O'Neill's *League of Extraordinary Gentlemen* series.

With this in mind, having been a true devotee of The Master of English Humour since the age of twelve, having engorged myself on his ridiculous 100+ volume-strong lifetime's output by the age of twenty, my mind often fell into the great man's idyllic universe, and demanded the question: what's happening there now? Given the fact that the poor chap has been dead for nearly 50 years, the answer should of course be 'nothing', but if we were to say that his universe was real, and we were living in it, what capers would be chronicled there in the twenty-first century, as we survive through the centenary of the Roaring Twenties?

As Britain dragged itself screaming through the 2010s, and fascism showed its frankly unattractive face all over the world in a way it had not dared do in all my lifetime, this question took on a different light, perhaps a different urgency. It came powered by a minuscule niggle which I had been almost unknowingly nursing and fulminating on since I was a child – the way in which it was so widely and automatically agreed among all lovers of The Master that one of his appeals is the escapism he offers from the real world, that the universe(s) he created were exquisitely executed candy floss farces and romances, a million miles from the realities of the early twentieth century.

Of course, this is overwhelmingly true, the comic universe in question was largely a silly paradise, but leaving aside the wonderful scholarly work which has been done by Norman T Murphy on finding some tangible real-world inspirations for The Master's many creations, wasn't there a glaring, giant, fascist fly in that literary consensus ointment? As the likes of Oswald Mosley marched over the horizon appealing to the very lowest instincts of humankind, bawling a philosophy so utterly opposite to the author's generally philanthropic spreading of sweetness and light – give or take the odd in-period-context blackface minstrel – what did this supposed fluffy fantasist do but roll up his sleeves and create a comic monster to set generations of readers laughing with disgust at the very idea of any jingoistic nonsense-spewing far-right hatemonger being taken seriously by decent folk. The 'Saviours of Britain' AKA the Black Shorts, were a pitch-perfect takedown of British fascism the best part of a century ago. And now, that piss-taking was required all over again.

Could that same form of mockery pull the same trick on the forces of bigotry in the 2020s?

Because now, as I looked around me, on social media and occasionally in real life, the descendants of that unforgettably revolting fictional villain seemed to be on the rise everywhere you looked. Who exactly was the modern-day version of that failed tin-pot dictator? And if he – for he-gammon they would surely be – was the antagonist, who would be the modern-day protagonist? Surely not some well-off toff with nothing to do with their lives but footle around and play golf. But if there's one class of citizen I do intimately know who can lead a laid back life perhaps analogous to that of the inter-war club man, it's musicians. The name 'Banjo' had also already appealed to me, a preferred rendering of 'Benjamin' and nothing whatsoever to do with replaying the game *Banjo Kazooie* at this time.

One thing suddenly seemed painfully obvious, though: whoever was to face off against this amalgam of Trump, Farage, Johnson and such dregs, they surely couldn't be a white straight man. And in fact, if this modern fascist was to pick on our hero... surely it would make sense that they would be Black? To make the hero some well-off white so-called "SJW-snowflake-virtue-signaller" type – or even a caucasian immigrant – may be more honest, coming from an author with absolutely no personal experience of life in Britain as an African refugee,

226

or as presenting as anything but a blotchy white. Besides the desire to present a diverse 2020s Britain, making the hero anything but visibly from an ethnic minority deflated so much of the central conflict of the whole concept.

Then there was far worse to come, of course – this wasn't just a case of hoping to present a positive multicultural Britain, as part of a light-hearted farcical narrative... this was a deliberate homage to an existing well-loved series of stories, and in all but one of those original narratives, the events were all documented by the protagonist. This had to be first-person. And I am not a half-Sudanese guy – nor, for that matter, by any means a half-English aristocratic guy. I have lived the life of a performer, I know my way around a festival stage, and I was brought up in a small town in the West Midlands. But it was ludicrous to imagine I could ever sufficiently empathise with a Black guy growing up in a white-dominated society, nor should I really attempt to, having obviously never been at the receiving end of systemic racism.

Above all, nothing should be done to in any way draw attention away from people of any racial heritage telling their own stories, providing authentic insight into just how racist our society has shamefully remained. And all of these realisations had been fully formed and worried over long before the news broke of the murder of George Floyd, and then, what's new? Before and after the rise of BLM, there have been an endless stream of injustices against Black people in the UK, the USA and the world over – now added to the stupendous insult that Covid-19 just happens to be twice as tough for Black people as white?

How could any decent person see all this unfolding from every news portal, both reliable and dodgy, and not get *angry*? The good heroes in The Master's universe never really got *angry*. A little piqued, perhaps – but then, they all wallowed in unquestioned privilege, and the aim of my creation was to present a parallel but very different modern update of that world.

There I was, attempting the already impossible task of trying to in some way write some light, jolly book which caught a millionth of the charm and sun-bathed joy of The Master's original stories, and suddenly, in the 2020s, it proved utterly impossible to keep the real world at bay. This was now a story about a care-free individual forced by the sheer piss-taking iniquity of modern Britain to become an activist, despite all his louche instincts.

When I asked myself – or of course, predicted others demanding to know – 'How the hell do you imagine you can capture the voice of a Black guy ten years younger than you?' – I of course knew it was hopeless. And yet, logically, how *dare* anyone suggest that there is a wrong voice or a right voice for anyone of any race, gender or place on spectrum of choice? Does he sound like Frank Bruno or Chris Eubank? Shirley Bassey or Richard Ayoade? It's logically absurd that anybody could dictate what anybody of any national or cultural heritage should sound like. If only the story which had taken hold of me could have taken hold in the mind of a different writer, less pink and stolidly so-called Celtic of descent! But our first-person narrator is a fellow from a small town who hasn't set foot in Southern Sudan since he was a baby – of course, his family would celebrate their African heritage, something which definitely required much education for me, but if this guy is just *who he is*... can he not just sound like himself? Besides, I was really rather growing to like the chap.

For my own selfish authorial reasons, by now the story had grown so much and so vividly, I found that I simply could not give up or go back, but I had to get the story told, all through numerous lockdowns, just in order to save myself a thousand long dark nights of the gut, regretfully taunting myself for my

228

literary cowardice. I always say, you should never start something you can't finish – end of.

And once written, surely my original experiment, to see if my favourite author's approach to taking on right-wing fascism with laughter was still possible today, could not be said to be completed unless... well, somebody actually read it? So some people did. And, having already published several books and spent some years deliberating over this light novel... It just seemed surreal not to publish a book that has absorbed so much life-force.

The fact remains, that this has been, perforce, an act of literary blackface. And that is simply not cool. And the fact that it was all done in the pursuit of spreading sweetness and light, paying – non-official and non-canonical – heartfelt tribute to the greatest joy-spreader in the history of English Literature, as a way of trying to deal with the darkness which has spread itself across world politics in the twenty-first century... is all just so much privileged pleading.

This, like every other book I have ever written, was created with zero expectation of financial profit, but any profits it ever ends up scraping together will be split equally with Waging Peace at wagingpeace.info – a charity helping Sudanese refugees build new lives over here in the UK.

As The Master said, "As we grow older and realise more clearly the limitations of human happiness, we come to see that the only real and abiding pleasure in life is to give pleasure to other people."

JFRS 2024

*Paperback copies of this novel may well be available. Please email jfrstableford@gmail.com if you would like one on your shelf.*